Special Th...

Thank you to all my family and friends for the love and support of my very first book. Without the encouragement and love, this may not have been possible. Many wanted this to become a reality and here is, the fruit of my labor. Thank you to those who helped me edit and gave insight on my storyline.
Thank you for everything.

Author's Disclaimer

This book is from the warped mind of a deranged author. The author does not care about your feelings, your mental stability, or ability to comprehend what you are about to read. This book is going to challenge and instigate many feelings that you have. The darkness in which brewed inside of the author's mind would scare, intimidate, and quite possibly kill anyone who tries to enter the mind of this harbinger of evil. Many have tried to understand what is going on in the author's mind, his psyche, and what dark world is in his mind. Never try to understand what is going on with the author. Only try to understand what you are reading, for you will never look at books the same again.

If you have strong convictions, this book is not for you. You might even change your religion after reading this book. This book will warp your mind, scare you, and could trigger many feelings you've never felt before.

The story your imagination is about to embark on is highly destructive to your childhood. You must leave morals, values, beliefs, and anything you hold dear outside this book. The world the author has created is mind-bending, sick, morbid, and dangerous. He advises if you have strong convictions to consider that this story may destroy everything you believe to be holy. This work of art is written by a person who wrote this book with unimpeded imagination and detail. What you imagine before, during, and after will give you an insight to the madness that lies in the mind of this author. The pure evil that courses through the eyes, mind, and body of this author would turn anyone "corpse white."

If you so doubt your ability to read anything that would open your eyes to a whole new side of literature, look deep in yourself to embrace the dark side of literature. Give into a world that is filled with darkness, violence, sex, and bloodshed. You will feel the embrace of the author as he grasps your interest, attention, and provoke your imagination until it is too much to handle.

Enjoy this tale of terror and immerse yourself in this dark world of the author's imagination. For more tales are soon to arise.

–

The Old Text

According to old text, the black ginger root is powerful, for it is used in black magic and is cursed. It is also known as black root, nightmare root, shadow root, and dead. This is a black-colored, magical root of unknown origin. If prepared and used correctly, it can do wonders. If not prepared correctly or is contaminated by human fluids or solids, it can have dangerous results. The root can heal wounds; bring once living beings back to life, even with indirect touch. This root can absorb a curse, hex, or enchantment, and amplify an effect in a negative way. It is never recommended to use this root under any circumstances; even if you are a professional harvester. Bare skin must never contaminate the root or it must be destroyed. A black ginger root can already have absorbed a curse, hex, or enchantment and pass it through direct skin contact. The only place to find this root is in the Pine Grove of the Mystic Forest. If you see black ginger roots sticking out of the ground, leave it be. It is not recommended that animals eat it either. Most wild creatures know to never eat this root, but domestic creatures do not know better. Even a touch from the root can forever curse an animal, and they will have an eternity of suffering ahead. To handle this root is to be damned. Heed this warning and never approach, touch, or eat this root. The only way to remove its negative effects is to burn the root that made contact with you in fire. Never let it make contact with the ground after it has touched you. or else the effects are permanent; for the root will cleanse itself and become a new root as it embeds itself into the ground.

Dark Times

In these dark times, punishments are way different from what they are today. If you are found guilty of committing certain atrocities to mankind, you may be transformed into an animal. If you come across a talking animal, especially in this time and age, you are encountering an animal that was once a human. Typically what happens if you cross anybody who performs dark arts or uses black magic in any sort of way, you can be transformed into an animal of their choice. If you are eating certain herbs, roots, or play with any sort of cursed item you could be transformed into an animal, object, or state of existence that it sees fit. That is why, in these times, it is better to be a good person than to be a criminal, a con artist, rapist, or just in general a bad person. Never underestimate the power of black magic, for it could be your undoing and you being permanently transformed for the rest of your days. Any ordinary animal that you come across will act as nature intended. But any "cursed animals," as they are called, will move and act irregularly compared to their natural animal brethren. Unless these cursed creatures practice black magic, they are forever cursed and cannot undo what has been done to them, for only the one who had cursed them can. No one is forgiving at this time and age. Once you have fallen victim to becoming a creature there is no coming back. Never cross the ones of darkness, for you have now been warned.

Chapter 1 – Mystic Forest

Our story begins deep in the Mystic Forest. Trees grow crooked and are covered in overgrowth. Only one path exists, and it's not a path you want to be on. As you pass through this path of uncertainty, there is no telling what is lurking around each corner. At the end of this path a light reveals a small house made of candy and sweets. This house is inviting, charming, and quaint. The outside edge of this property is lined with trees and overgrowth with a beautiful array of tulips, daisies, and lavender lining the base of the trees. On the side of the house is a small wood pile for the chimney. What is on the inside isn't so quaint. For in this house is a crazed old woman who lures people, mainly children, into her house of terror. Inside is a clean little kitchen in the front, but when you pass down the hallway there is a series of locked doors with no telling what horrors lie behind them. When you pass through the hallway there is a piercing stench of rotting flesh, urine, and feces. For one of these doors is a prison cell with no windows, fresh air, or a way out. This crazed old woman loves the taste of flesh, the sounds of pain and suffering, and the smell of decay. She also loves to lure men into her home then kill, skin, and devour them. This crazed old woman loves her human pelts that she has hand sewn in her down time after she has tanned them. She also loves to cut off men's genitalia, hollow it out, and insert a hand carved phallus after she tanned the skin, then she will name each one for her pleasure. This was her favorite hobby and her most prized possessions.

This crazed old woman has scarred skin, a bent nose, graying skin, thin white hair, and is all skin and bones.. This woman is near death and under constant torment from her curse. For you see, she does forbidden rituals that involve killing and consuming children to absorb their life energies. She harvests children by means of kidnapping and abduction practice. When she sees an opportunity, she will even abduct babies as they sleep in their bassinets. When she learns of a new child being born, she will wait for the opportune moment to seize the infant and stash them away for her selfish needs. Her methods include putting the children in cages, towers, and even caves with the only way to escape is the way in which you came in. All in her plan to live forever.

This crazed old woman makes her clothes from remnants of cloth from the children's clothing that she kidnaps and consumes. Nothing is left to waste when she harvests the children's corpses. She will use the skin for leather and disguises, the muscle she will prepare for long storage and consumption, and she will grind the bones into a fine powder for part of her rituals. She will even snort the bone powder as a form of meditation. She has even perfected a process to ferment bone and blood to make her own liquor. She hates small animals and will kill them for their pelts, flesh, and bone for the same reasons. The crazed old woman will use flesh remnants to repair her broken skin, like patches on trousers. Many glass jars lay in storage full of human parts for her personal use to sustain life.

One day the crazed old woman found a lost little girl out in the Mystic Forest. She dashed to a nearby bush and waited until Gretel came close. Stricken with fear Gretel had forgotten which direction she came from. So the crazed old woman had a change of heart. She emerged from the bushes and greeted Gretel, "Hello young lady. Are you lost?" Gretel jumped back as she was startled by the presence of the old woman. Gretel had no idea where she was and couldn't find her way back. "Yes," replied Gretel, "I have no idea where I am and I am so scared." Gretel began to cry and the crazed old woman became aroused. While Gretel was sobbing the crazed old woman's mouth began to salivate and she raised her hand and placed it on Gretel's head. The crazed old woman pulled Gretel in close for a hug, "Let me help you young lady," said the crazed old woman, "You look scared, hungry, and cold. Come with me." Gretel didn't hesitate and followed the woman to her house.

Earlier that day

This lost little girl is named Gretel Haushgutt. She and her family were out on a nice ride on the family horse and buggy. Gretel's father, Timothy Haushgutt, her mother, Helga Haushgutt, and her one-year-old baby brother, Hans Haushgutt, were on their way to go circle the Mystic Forest as a family trip. Timothy thought it would be a hilarious joke to scare the family with the strange noises of the Mystic Forest. They were singing their favorite songs on the way up while Helga was also reading stories to the children. Everyone was enjoying the trip. "Hey everyone, we have arrived," said Timothy. Helga finished the last sentence in her book and the whole family faced the Mystic Forest. "Look Gretel, those trees are so old they are almost impossible to cut down," said Helga, "your grandfather told me he tried to cut one of the younger trees when he was 30-years-old and could not." "Wow mommy," said Gretel, "how does that happen?" "Well honey, these trees are so old they were around longer than a lot of trees we see today," said Helga, "instead of getting larger, the trees become almost rock hard. Some even say harder than diamonds. But these are just legends." "I like those stories mommy," said Gretel, "what else can you tell me about the trees?" Timothy interrupts, "Everyone quiet! I don't think we are alone." Timothy carefully scans the tree line and out into the meadow surrounding the Mystic Forest.

Timothy was laughing to himself and trying not to give away his plan. For you see, he paid his friend a few gold pieces to go into the mystic forest 20 minutes ahead of them. Timothy wanted to scare his family because of the rumors surrounding the Mystic Forest. He heard some light crackling of tree branches just beyond the tree line and light growling. In Timothy's mind, he thought everything was going to plan and his family would have a big laugh about this. He doesn't realize what is actually beyond the tree line waiting for them. Timothy gave a thumbs up to the creature beyond the tree line, not knowing he was mistaking it for being his friend. All of a sudden something heavy hits Timothy in the lap and he wondered why it was wet. He looked down, only to find the head of his best friend in his lap, with a look of betrayal on his face. On quick inspection, it appears that Timothy's friend's head was not cut off, it was pulled off. The bloodstained skin and the look in the eyes of his friend's head will haunt Timothy for the rest of his days. Timothy looked back at where the creature was and noticed a black silhouette stand up on its hind legs. This enormous creature growled even louder than before and was inching closer. It was then, that Timothy realized they were being hunted and he needed to move.

"Everyone hold on tight," ordered Timothy, "that thing is not human and we need to get out of here immediately!" "What do you think it is?" asked Helga with a sense of panic in her voice. "I don't know, but it's massive and it doesn't look friendly," responded Timothy with a sense of fear. With a harsh snap of the reins, the horse took off with the buggy at full sprint. "I certainly hope this buggy holds together," whispered Timothy, "this thing is not meant for high-speeds like this." Timothy continued to monitor the creature beyond the tree line and it was keeping pace with the horse. With the sheer size of this creature it seemed like it was making effortless bounds to keep up with the horse. "Shit! That fucking thing is not backing down!" exclaimed Timothy, "I've got to lose it somehow." Timothy knew that if he suddenly stopped the horse and buggy, they would be killed. So his only course of action was to keep going straight and try to find a way to escape. He also remembered that the horse can only go so far before it gets tired. So many scenarios are going through Timothy's head yet all he can do is think about his

family. He stayed vigilant and determined to save his family from this horrific end.

Timothy peered over at the tree line and did not see the black silhouette anymore. His first instinct was telling him to slow down and turn around. Something was not right about this situation and his secondary instinct was screaming to keep moving forward. Timothy did not have the horse slow down and continued looking for a way to get them out of the situation. Seconds felt like hours and his heart was racing. Timothy looked back at his family and said, "I will get us out of this. Is everybody okay back there?" Gretel merely nodded and Helga said, "Yes." The baby was screaming in sheer terror because he had no idea what was going on. Helga and Gretel did everything they could to comfort the little one but it was doing no good. This experience will scar the child for the rest of his days.

Suddenly out of nowhere, with his teeth bearing, a giant wolf came out of the woodwork and attacked the horse. The horse was knocked on his side and the buggy rolled and snapped off the driving harness. Tragedy struck when Gretel and her baby brother were thrown from the buggy and their parents were killed by the buggy. During the role, Timothy and Helga were beheaded as the buggy rolled across their necks. You could not see the heads, because the buggy was lying on top of them. Their blood stained the top side of the buggy. Gretel looks on in horror as she sees her parent's lifeless bodies laying in the grass. She was paralyzed in fear and all she could do was hold her baby brother and watch as the horse is torn to shreds. The wolf is tearing the horse apart as if it hadn't eaten for a week. Taking huge bites of flesh out of the horses hide and crushing the bone between its mighty jaws, the wolf showed no mercy. As the wolf mauled the horse, digging its claws deep within its flesh, and breaking each bone, Gretel realized they were in grave danger.

Gretel looked down at her baby brother and realized he was dead. When they were thrown from the buggy he landed on the ground and broke his neck. Gretel was determined to give her little brother a proper burial, however she may not have a choice in the matter. The wolf could sense that there was a living being nearby and he began sniffing around. The wolf quickly realized that Gretel was the lone survivor and charged at her. Gretel stood up quickly, picked up her little brother, and ran towards the forest. The wolf did not follow Gretel, at least not now. The wolf had her scent and was ready to hunt her down once he was done with the rest of the family.

The wolf was extremely hungry and had to get enough food to give him the energy he would need to hunt down Gretel and her baby brother. He went back to the horse and began consuming flesh and bone. In the distance you can hear the bones cracking and crunching in the wolf's mighty jaws. Once he had finished with his appetizer, he started with his second course, Gretel's parents. Lifting up the buggy he picked up the heads and proceeded to eat them as if they were grapes. With his strong jaws he crunched down on their skulls with little to no effort. Tearing off the limbs one by one, the wolf sectioned the corpses of Timothy and Helga. Blood stained the surrounding grass as the wolf finished the remaining bits of Gretel's parents. The wolf licked his lips, smelled the air, and began tracking Gretel and her baby brother.

Gretel did not slow down her pace. She was determined to live and give her baby brother a proper burial. She figured that was the least she could give her little brother at this point. When Gretel began to feel the searing pain of exhaustion, she found a quiet spot in the forest and began to dig a hole to bury her baby brother. "I'm sorry Hans," said Gretel, "it was my job to protect you and I failed you. I am so sorry. Please forgive me, please." Gretel cried profusely because she felt guilty that she couldn't save her baby brother and he was the remaining family she had. "I love you Hans," cried Gretel, "may the Creator be merciful and bring you into his arms. Tell mom and dad I love them and I'll see you guys soon." The pain of loss for Gretel was becoming too much. She had lost her entire family in one attack and she didn't know what to do, so she continued to dig a grave for Hans.

When she finally finished digging a grave for Hans, she went to reach for him and he was gone. She began to frantically search for him because she promised him a proper burial. Then all of a sudden her skin ran cold when she realized she was not alone. A menacing shadow came over her and she slowly turned around. She realized the wolf had tracked her down and this meant the end for her. With Hans in the wolf's right hand, the wolf placed baby Hans inside of his mouth and proceeded to bite down on his lifeless body. Gretel looked on in horror as her baby brother was being eaten like a shrimp. Once the wolf swallowed baby Hans, he got on all fours, baring his mighty teeth, and crept menacingly towards Gretel. Gretel's heart began racing out of control. She thought she was going to pass out. Suddenly, she grabbed a handful of loose dirt and threw it into the eyes of the wolf, temporarily blinding him. The wolf snarled and frantically tried to clear his eyes so his prey would not get away. Gretel then picked up a rock, about the size of a cat's head, and threw it at the wolf's face. With a direct hit to the wolf's nose, the wolf's eyes began to water and a sharp pain was piercing his face. Gretel stood up and ran as quickly as she could deeper into the forest.

During her escape from the Wolf, she came across an unnerving swamp. The swamp glowed with an eerie gray hue. Various animal corpses line the shoreline of scattered pools of diseased water and the creek shoreline. The smell of death and rotting flesh pierced through the air. As Gretel breathes the air, it burns her throat and nostrils; it makes her eyes water and vision blurs. Gretel quickly learned to mind the soft spots in the ground. The soft spots may be a decayed corpse covering up a small pool of water or quicksand. Some pools are completely covered with decay that anyone may be sucked to the very bottom of the swamp, never to be seen again. This swamp is known for animals coming here to die. Many come to die here because they are sick, old, or dying. The bones of the animals litter the floor and banks of the creek to be forgotten.

The trees are ancient and lifeless. Gretel noticed the unease the trees create with leafless branches and entangled where little to no light may show through. She saw a film that hung on the branches that looked torn white silk. Some looked like decaying curtains in an abandoned home. Insects, arachnids, and centipede-like creatures scurry and feast on remains of different creatures flesh. With the presence of rotting flesh around they scavenge and pick corpses clean. Gretel looks on in horror as she bears witness to this grotesque scene.

As Gretel continued to walk through the swamp, she noticed there were no birds singing. The sounds present here are occasional gas bubbles bursting in the pools or through the creek that runs through the swamp. If you stay long enough, you may bear witness to an animal die and listen to it's final sounds of demise.

In this swamp, there was a small hut made out of straw and mud. From the hut something yell angrily, "Beat it or I will kill you." It almost sounded like a pig squeal mixed with a human voice. Gretel swiftly exited the area. During her travels, she came across two more huts one made out of wood and one made out of brick. Gretel did not dare go inside because the area was unfamiliar to her. She suddenly heard the angry grunts of boars all around her and she knew she was in danger. She ran as quickly as she could without hesitation. Gretel's adrenaline was pulsating through her entire being and she frantically tried to get away from danger.

Gretel was hoping to find a clear path to walk on because she had been running through the trees and overgrowth for what seemed to be hours. Conveniently she found a clear path and she became more hopeful, despite losing her entire family. Her survival could mean the survival for many people. Gretel planned to have the wolf killed once she was able to find help. For now she would settle for someone to give her shelter temporarily. While on the path Gretel found some berries, edible bugs, and fungus to restore some of her strength. Though she was very grateful, it was not enough food. Her desperation traveled throughout the Mystic Forest and began to attract unwanted attention.

Present time

While walking down the path, Gretel noticed the woman was always peering down at her. "Why do you keep looking at me like that?" asked Gretel. The crazed old woman quickly looked back up then she looked back down at Gretel and asked, "Um, what do you mean my dear?" Gretel responded, "Why do you keep looking at me like that? You keep looking at me instead of looking forward." The crazed old woman playfully said, "Oh my child, you have been through so much. I am just making sure you are okay and feel safe. Is there something wrong with an old granny looking out for a little one, such as yourself?" Gretel hesitated, "Well…I guess not. But why are you licking your lips when you look at me?" Again the crazed old woman said playfully, "My dear, I am old and these old lips don't work like they used to. You'll be old before you know it." Gretel smiled and said, "Hopefully not too soon. I like being a kid." Gretel reached for the old woman's hand and held it. Gretel began to trust the horrid old woman. "Is your house much farther ma'am," asked Gretel. "It's just up this way my dear and around the corner," said the crazed old woman.

They soon turned the corner and in an open space with rays of sunshine beaming down sat a small house made of candy. Gretel couldn't believe her eyes on how beautiful the site was. She slowly stepped closer to the house just to bask in the beauty of the house's majesty. "How did you make this house," asked Gretel, "this place is so pretty." The crazed old woman responded, "Thank you my dear. I didn't build it. Many wonderful people helped this old granny build this place. They were rewarded for their hard work."

Inside the mind of the sick crazed old woman: *She had fed those who helped her poisoned food and treats to paralyze her victims so they would be alive but couldn't fight back. She butchered several people who helped her. She removed their* *skin, cut off their muscle tissue, and taunted them as they slowly died. When the men had erections after their body died, she cut off the penis and kept it as a keepsake. She bathed in their blood and ate raw flesh as if she had not eaten in over a year. The fear in the eyes of the people she murdered in cold blood, made her aroused and she began to place her hands on her body and caress everywhere she could touch. She would scream into their dying faces, tormenting them and scoring their skin with her long, filthy talons to inflict pain. She plunged her long fingernails into the eyeballs of the victims and all you could hear was a light moan of pain. Curling her fingers she would remove the eyes from their sockets and proceed to devour each one in front of those still conscious. Flesh flying everywhere, bodily organs ripped from the still living bodies, pain inflicted, and she laughed as her victims slowly died painfully around her…………………*

"They did a great job," said Gretel, "I hope one day I can meet them for my dream home." The crazed old woman looked at Gretel and with a sadistic smile said, "Oh I have a feeling you will meet them very soon. You will be given the same treatment they received and more." Gretel was so excited she ran towards all the flowers and ran around the house. "It smells like Heaven!" exclaimed Gretel, "I never want to leave."

Inside the mind of the crazed old woman:
"You'll never leave. You little shit!" The crazed old woman blades her hand and slaps Gretel across her

face and the girl's neck cracks loudly with five cracks. Gretel falls to the ground and her body randomly starts twitching and is unable to move under her own power. "You will never leave this place. You are now my prisoner. You cannot resist me now you foolish little bitch." Dragging Gretel's semi lifeless body into the house and…………

"This is a paradise little girl. Now you must be hungry. Let us head inside for some delicious food and treats," said the crazed old woman. "I have chocolate from far off lands, sweets from the local town, and food out of my garden. Oh, I must not forget, I am roasting a delicious duck on the fireplace." Gretel's eyes lit up and she exclaimed, "I haven't eaten in ages, could we please have some food, ma'am?" The crazed old woman looked at her with a confident smile, "Yes let's…eat." They walked up to the door and the crazed old woman opened the door. Gretel went inside without hesitation, the crazed old woman walked in with a victorious smile, and with a sadistic giggle she closed the door, she locked the door behind her. "Have a seat at the table my dear," said the crazed old woman, "I have some delicious duck roasting over the fire." Gretel was very excited to hear that she was about to eat a delicious roast duck. So Gretel had a seat at the table and had a look around the room. "You have a very nice house here ma'am," said Gretel, "it looks like an average kitchen compared to what the outside of your house looks like." The crazed old woman looked at Gretel and said, "Well I like my house to be very inviting, especially for small children."

Chapter 2 – A Random Act of Deceit

Haunting memory surfaces in the mind of the crazed old woman

Shrouded in a cloak, her face visible, the crazed old woman walks into a candy shop with her basket in hand. She looks around the shop seeking the most delicious-looking treats in the land. As she makes her way around the shop, the shopkeeper asks, "Hello ma'am. Is there anything I can help you find today?" The crazed old woman replies with her scratchy voice trying to sound polite, "I'm just browsing young man, but rest assured I will ask you if I need something or need to see something." The young shopkeeper just smiled and bowed his head in respect. The shopkeeper could not be more than 16 years old and the crazed old woman could pick up on his youth, his ignorance, and his trusting nature. The crazed old woman continued to gather all the goods that she wanted in her basket.

"You have a lot of goodies in here young man," said the crazed old woman, 'I wish my house could be made out of all this." The shopkeeper looked at her and giggled slightly, "That would be quite a sight to see ma'am. Honestly, I would love to see something like that." The crazed old woman turned around slowly and asked, "Really? Well you're in luck my handsome young lad; my house actually is made out of candy." Confused, the young man replied, "What?" With nothing but malice in her mind she grins sadistically, "Yes…My house is made out of candy, you should come see it." Curious young shopkeeper thought to himself, "This is impossible, it would never hold up under all that weight. Plus candy isn't strong enough to be used as a structure." So many questions are running through his head, like, "is this old woman crazy? Does she know something I don't? Could such a house actually exist? Is this old woman drunk? Is she using that candy to make some sort of drug?"

"What time does your shop close young man," asked the crazed old woman, "I would be more than happy to show you my candy house. I don't get many visitors because I live out in the middle of the forest. It's quite a hike for an old woman like me. Would you like to honor me with your presence and give me a few hours of your company?" The young shopkeeper hesitated, but was very intrigued by what he is being told, for he had never seen a candy house before and he thought it had to be cosmetic, not real. Against his better judgment he told the old woman, "well ma'am we close in about an hour or so. I suppose I could spare a few hours to check out your home. Where exactly is it located?" The crazed old woman looked at him and said "It's in the Mystic Forest. Do you happen to have a carriage or a horse that can pull a buggy?" The young shopkeeper said, "As a matter of fact I do have a horse and buggy that we can use to get to your home."

An hour passed and the young shopkeeper locked the doors of the shop. He hitched up his horse and buggy and assisted the crazed old woman on to the buggy. Along the way to the crazed old woman's house, the unlikely couple shared some laughs, life stories, and a few life experiences with each other. Once they arrived at the old woman's candy house, the young shopkeeper was amazed at what he saw. "I cannot believe my eyes! This is beyond amazing," the young shopkeeper rambled on, "how is this even possible? I can smell the gingerbread walls, the peppermint, the gumdrops, and the icing! This is impossible. How did you even get candy that big?" The house wasn't that big but it was still quite impressive to this young man who had been in the candy industry all his life. "Would you like to come in and see the inside, my dear?" The crazed old woman asked very gingerly, "I'm going to need some help getting these treats organized inside." Mesmerized by this beautiful site, the young man helps the old woman off the buggy, hands her the basket of goodies, and assists her to the house. The crazed old woman gave him instruction on what to do and where to put everything. Little did the young man know his life was very quickly coming to an end. The crazed old woman grabbed an old femur bone she had hidden in a drawer across the room. The young shopkeeper had his back turned to the crazed old woman, not knowing what she was up to; for he was focused on helping this deceivingly nice old lady. This young man was so focused on his task that the crazed old woman crept up on him slowly and patiently. She knew that he had plenty to do and she had more than enough time to execute her plan. With one final step, she raises the femur up over her head with both hands, takes aim, draws back, and before she could swing, the young man starts to turn around. The crazed old woman quickly hides the bone behind her back with one hand and reaches up with her other hand and caresses the young man's cheek. "You have been such a big help," said the crazed old woman, "why don't you have a seat at the kitchen table and I will make you a delicious meal." The young man was astounded by the generosity of this old woman. He had never been treated so well in his life or even invited to another person's house. Not many people have accepted him into their lives nor did he have any family left to visit, for this young man, like the crazed old woman, lives alone and has no living relatives or any friends.

The old crazed woman quickly stashed the femur bone back in the drawer where she had it stored. She did not want to give away her plan at this point in time. Instead she grabbed a sharpened utensil out of the drawer which looked like an ordinary knife but it wasn't. She went over to her cutting board and began slicing some bread for the young man and grabbed him some butter, cinnamon, and sugar. "Help yourself, young man," said the crazed old woman, "for I have something in my kettle over my fireplace." As the young man was buttering his toast and sprinkling a light amount of cinnamon and sugar, the crazed old woman went over to the kettle with a bowl and ladle and scooped out some soup into the bowl. The crazed old woman's mouth begins to salivate because her intentions are not only wicked but sexual. As she walks back to the table she draws the knife, which is merely a sharpened human rib, and rams the rib into the back of the young shopkeeper, piercing his left lung. As the blood fills his lung, he begins to panic from the searing pain in his body. As he tries to stand up and run, the crazed old woman severs his Achilles tendon and begins to laugh. "You little fool," said the crazed old woman, "you are going to give me something I need right now. Whether you're alive or not I'm gonna get my hands on it." The young man, unable to respond in speech, could only imagine what this old woman was going to do to him.

The crazed old woman thrusts the sharpened rib multiple times into the young shopkeeper's thighs hitting both arteries. The young shopkeeper is now suffocating and bleeding to death from his legs. "Now before I devour you, I'm going to cut your penis off and I'm gonna use it to flavor my soup," cackled the crazed old woman. She takes her sharpened rib, cuts off his belt, slices his pants and underwear in one swipe near his groin area, grabs a hold of his penis, and with one swipe, cuts off his testicles and penis. The young shopkeeper tries to scream but all that could be heard is gurgling and the sound of blood coming out of his mouth. He begins to hyperventilate and all he is doing is pumping blood into his other lung and slowly dying. The crazed old woman sat down where the young man was previously and used the young man's penis as a straw to slurp up the soup. She siphons the soup through his urethra from the bowl to her mouth. With one final gurgle the young man was no more. The crazed old woman later on butchered the young man and cleaned up her house for her next victim. She gathered all the butchered pieces and placed them in old jars. She then stored them away for another day for any dastardly purpose she deems necessary. Smiling provocatively, she stores the penis in her room for later that night.

<u>Chapter 3 – A Chance of Freedom</u>

The crazed old woman snaps out of her daydream

"You must be hungry my dear," said the crazed old woman, "let me grab you that duck I promised." The crazed old woman walks over to the fireplace where the duck is cooking. "The duck is finished and just in the nick of time," said the crazed old woman, "this is an old recipe that's older than I am." Gretel was very excited to try this duck that was made especially for her. Gretel had no idea what she was getting herself into. The crazed old woman placed the duck on the table and began parting the duck. "Do you want a wing, a breast, a leg, or a thigh," asked the crazed old woman, "you are my guest, you have first choice." Gretel picked a breast. "Now eat up my child, I will go get something out of my garden," said the crazed old woman. But the crazed old woman was not going to get anything out of her garden. Instead, she went to retrieve a large femur bone out of a drawer in the kitchen. The crazed old woman wishes to render Gretel unconscious so she is fresh for later.

The crazed old woman begins creeping up behind Gretel, she raises the femur with two hands, takes aim, and swings with all her might at the back of Gretel's head; knocking Gretel unconscious. The crazed old woman drags Gretel into a dark room with no windows and only one door. In this room was a homemade cage that the crazed old woman made. The crazed old woman drug the twitching little girl into the room, placed her body inside of the cage, closed the door, and locked it. "You my dear are going to be a delicious meal for me in the next few days. So get comfortable because you're going nowhere," cackled the crazed old woman.

Gretel had been unconscious for hours and when she came to she could not see anything.. The room was pitch black as if she were blind. She couldn't hear any sounds outside except the sounds that she made. The smell in this room was horrible. Acrid smells of rotting flesh, feces, and despair filled the room. "Where am I?" thought Gretel in horror. She began to feel around the floor inside the cage trying to find a way out. But all Gretel felt was a damp, slippery wood floor but when she moved away from the wall she felt the bars of the cage. She then realized they too were made of wood. So Gretel began kicking at the weak spots she found in the cage. With each kick she could hear crackle and she would feel it with her hands to check on her progress. She kicked at the cage for hours and suddenly the cage door opened up. Gretel felt around the room to find the door handle but she could not find one. For the crazed old woman had removed the door handle on that side of the door.

Gretel decided, out of desperation, to begin kicking whatever she could as hard as she could, yelling and screaming, and possibly getting the attention of the crazed old woman. Hours went by with no luck of getting that old woman to open the door. Gretel put her ear up to what she thought was the door and could hear footsteps coming her way. "Yes," Gretel thought, "she's finally coming my way." The sound of a key entering a keyhole and turning to open the door echoed through the small damp room. As the door slowly opened, light began to fill the room and revealed the horrors that Gretel could not see before. She saw skeletons of small children all over the room, children's dolls and toys nailed to the wall, arms and legs of small children hanging from the ceiling like meat at a butcher shop. Gretel tried not to vomit from the horror that she has been exposed to. The crazed old woman entered the room and walked towards the cage then realized that Gretel had escaped. Gretel ran out of the room trying to find her way out of the house.

"GET BACK HERE!" shrieked the crazed old woman chasing Gretel. Gretel was trying to escape her hellish prison in the woods. Running through the house made of candy trying every door yet all were locked. She stumbled upon an open door, ran inside, and slammed it shut. The room is cold, dark, damp, and smells of rotting flesh. "Help," whispered a little boy, "Help me, please. She's going to eat me next." Gretel looked around the room and she could see faint movement in the back left corner of the room with the sound of chains scraping and clunking across the wooden floor. "What is that sound?" asked Gretel. The boy responded, "They're my chains. She has them long enough so I can eat off the floor." "Oh my god," Gretel quietly exclaimed, "what is that awful smell?" "I was forced to eat dead rats, birds, and what I think is rotted flesh." said the boy sobbing. "Flesh of what?" asked Gretel. "I don't want to say," said the boy. Gretel felt a chill down her spine and grew cold. "You mean.....human....flesh?" asked Gretel. The boy covered his eyes in shame, his body began to shake, and began to cry and said, "Yes...human flesh. I have been starved for days at a time and given little to no water. I had to drink my pee to survive and occasionally eat my......" the boy couldn't finish his story. He began to feel scared and sick. Gretel said, "You do not need to tell me anymore. Let me help you. Where is the key to your chains?" The boy responded, "I think that sick old cunt keeps the key inside her cookbook in the kitchen. She uses it as a bookmark for each kid she eats." Feeling a sudden rush of courage, Gretel looked at the boy and said, "Ok, I am going to get that key, which book is it?" The boy felt calmer and said, "It's a hardcover black book. It has blood stains on the pages and there's a sewn in purple ribbon under the front cover. The title is unknown to me. It's in some foreign language." Gathering her courage Gretel looked at the boy and said, "Listen to me; we are getting out of her together. Okay? We are getting out of this awful place together." The boy responded, "Ok......Together."

One Week Ago

This young boy and his father went to the market to buy food for the little boy's birthday party.

The young boy goes by the name Hanzel Beznacht and his father Jan Beznacht. During their shopping adventure, Hanzel notices a strangely dressed mysterious person in the market. This person was covered in animal furs, odd looking leather, and wore a hood that made the face impossible to see. Hanzel couldn't help but feel he was being watched by this person. When he looked at his father to tell him about the mysterious person, the mysterious person vanished from sight. Hanzel became very uneasy and started looking around frantically but there was no sign of the mysterious person. Little did Hanzel know, his life was about to change forever. Jan noticed that his son was shaking in fear; he turned and asked Hanzel, "My son, what is wrong? Please tell me what happened." Hanzel continued to look around and his voice was quivering trying to tell his father what had happened. Jan got down on one knee and hugged his son, "Don't worry my boy. Nothing will harm you as long as I'm with you." Hanzel gripped his father tight and said, "I saw a mysterious person that was dressed in fur and leather. I believe they were after me or were watching me as I walked with you." Puzzled, Jan looked around the marketplace and did not see this mysterious individual that Hanzel spoke of. "Hanzel, no one is out there nor going to get you," said Jan, "now let's finish the shopping so we can get ready for your party."

Jan and Hanzel continued to walk through the market and peruse the many shops. Jan wants to make sure that Hanzel had the perfect birthday that he'll never forget. Jan purchased some various activities for the party including: croquet, dice, ring

toss, and even a massive custom-made schultüte.
Hanzel's schultüte was made from paper with all his
favorite colors: blue, black, and orange. This cone
shaped delight was as tall as Hanzel and was a little
too heavy for him to carry. With a delighted chuckle
Jan said to Hanzel, "Allow me to open this my son. It
is heavier than I thought it was going to be." Hanzel
smiled and handed the schultüte to his father.

    On the way home, Jan and Hanzel stopped at
the local bakery and picked up the birthday cake.
Hanzel can't wait for the party to begin and he didn't
care if there were any decorations. All he just wants
is to have fun with this family and friends. Hanzel
asked his father if he could see what the cake looks
like but Jan said that he had to wait until the party.
Hanzel's excitement grew as the seconds ticked by.

    All day at home, Jan worked diligently to
make sure that everything was ready for when the
guests arrived. Jan looked on as his only son, Hanzel,
was helping to finish the decorating before the guests
arrived. They both knew that they needed to stick
together and push through; so they could become
stronger for each other. For you see, Hanzel had a
rough year with the loss of his mother. Hanzel's
mother died of a mysterious illness that doctors could
not figure out. All Hanzel knew is that his mother was
in pain, and wished to pass on to get rid of the pain.
In her final moments of life, the only thing she
regretted was not being able to watch her son grow
up into a man.

As the mid afternoon sun shined upon the party, everyone was having the time of their lives. The guests were impressed with the decorations, the food, and all the hard work that Hanzel and his father put into this party. No one could believe that an 11-year-old would be so willing to help out for their own party. Everyone in town showed up for this momentous occasion because they want to show their love and support for the Beznacht family. Not everyone was there to celebrate and join in the festivities. The mysterious person followed them from the market to their home. Mysterious person had a dastardly plan that they desperately needed to fulfill. So they hid inside the basement of the house and waited till everyone was asleep.

After the festivities had come to a close, Hanzel fell asleep outside in the garden. Jan picked him up and carried Hanzel to his bedroom. Hanzel had never had so much fun in his life and would remember for the rest of his life. After placing Hanzel in his bed for the night, Hanzel's father kissed him goodnight…for the last time. The mysterious person moved cautiously through the house and searched for Hanzel's room. Opening each door very cautiously, the mysterious person scans the rooms one by one and searches for obvious signs of a child's room. Looking for any stuffed animals, sporting equipment, toys, etc. this person was on a serious mission and time was running out.

The mysterious person finally came upon Hanzel's room and quietly entered. As they crept *slowly towards Hanzel's bed, they pulled out a small leather bag with a string tie, and prepared to execute their plan. Inside of the small leather bag, was a powder that slows one's heart rate to near death for 3 days. The average doctor during this era would presume death or near death and would recommend a funeral. But the mysterious thing about the powder is that once it wears off, your heart rate returns to normal. Although rare, there have been incidents of people dying from using this powder on themselves or other people. The mysterious person sprinkled the powder on the Hanzel's face and it quickly absorbed into the skin. Shortly after the powder touched the skin, Hanzel became cold as a corpse, and lay motionless and barely breathing.*

The next morning, Jan calls Hanzel for breakfast but there was no response. Jan approaches Hanzel's bedroom, opens the door, and attempts to wake the young boy. Hanzel's father checks Hanzel's pulse on his wrist, but he couldn't feel his pulse. He checks his heart by placing his ear to Hanzel's chest, but he couldn't hear a heartbeat. Distraught and panicking, Jan yells for help, "Someone help me, my son is dying." The local doctor just happened to be in the neighborhood and followed Jan up to the room to see Hanzel. The doctor declared Hanzel dead and made a trip down to the morgue to inform the mortician of Hanzel's passing. Hanzel's body was transported to the morgue where he was prepped for his funeral. The mysterious person had snuck in with the presumed dead body of Hanzel. No one noticed the mysterious person as they hid in a closet and waited until nightfall. The mortician placed Hanzel's body in the coffin Jan picked out for him and started to clean the mortuary.

Once the mortician finished cleaning and locked up for the night, the mysterious person came out of hiding and walked over to Hanzel's helpless body. They pulled out the little leather bag and sprinkled more of the dust on Hanzel's face. "This will ensure you will stay asleep," said the mysterious person, "soon you'll be my prisoner and will be consuming your flesh before you know it." The mysterious person opened the coffin entirely and examined Hanzel's body. "You look like a tender little morsel. I can't wait to sink my teeth into your flesh," said the mysterious person, "but I will let your friends and family say their goodbyes first." The mysterious person resumed their plan by hiding back in the closet and waiting for nightfall once again.

That night, Jan was in such distress he began drinking heavily. He cried and started talking to every object in the house about how he lost his whole family. Jan was talking to the furniture and other inanimate objects as if they were people surrounding him. The stress had overcome him and he eventually blacked out from his drunken haze. Jan had become more than intoxicated; he became mentally ill from all the stress.

The next morning the mortician set up the room for friends and family to visit Hanzel and opened the mortuary before his burial. He was also puzzled that Hanzel's coffin was wide open. He could've sworn that he had closed it before he left for the night. The mortician did not have time to think, for there were a lot of people coming to pay their respects today. The whole town showed up to show their respects and to help comfort Jan in his time of need. Because the whole town showed up to pay their respects to Jan and the "recently deceased," Hanzel, the mortician moved the burial to the next day. After the last person left the mortuary, the mortician again cleaned up and locked up for the night. Once the mysterious person heard the lock on the door click, they waited a few additional minutes to ensure no one would come back. The mysterious person came out of the closet, walked over to Hanzel's coffin and began to salivate. The mysterious person removed the hood from over there head, looked at Hanzel's body, and became extremely aroused at her latest victim. The mysterious person that had been stalking Hanzel, was a crazed old woman that didn't have a name. All that was on her mind was how tasty he was going to be on a spit. "Come with me little man," said the crazed old woman, "you are going to be my dinner and you are going to be delicious. I hope your friends and family like the surprise I left them in your coffin."

Without alerting anyone, the crazed old woman stole Hanzel's body from the mortuary, and placed his lifeless body in her cart and covered his body with the extra fur she had. The crazed old woman transported Hanzel to her house in the Mystic Forest. Along the way, she was coming up with recipes she could use to prepare his body for dinner.

But she would need to consult her black cookbook to find the perfect recipe.

Once she arrived at her home in the Mystic Forest, the crazed old woman grabbed Hanzel by his upper jaw and drug him to a dark room. She abruptly dropped Hanzel's head on the floor and his head made a thunderous thud on the floor which echoed through the room. She proceeded to shackle him to the wall while laughing sadistically. "No one will ever miss you," said the crazed old woman to the unconscious Hanzel, "you will be joining your family soon enough. Then with the slam of a door and a turn of the key, Hanzel was now her prisoner.

The next morning was supposed to be Hanzel's funeral and burial. But little did Hanzel's friends and family realize, the crazed old woman left a sack of rabid rodents in the coffin. These rodents are not your typical rodents, they are 2 feet long and weigh about 4 pounds. They look like beefy rats with long, razor-sharp teeth. If they do not feed within two days, they will viciously attack and kill anything to get a meal. They have a very violent temperament, especially when they don't feed for long periods of time and become bloodthirsty. The crazed old woman drugged these rodents and did not feed them for four days. Essentially, they are beyond the point of no return and will feed on any living flesh-bearing creature. Another thing to know about these rodents is never startle them even when they have fed because they are very defensive animals as well.

Jan opens the coffin to say his last goodbye to his baby boy, the light hits the eyes of the rodents. Without hesitation, the rodents leapt at Jan and any nearby guests and began to feed on the flesh. Using their sharp claws they tear through the facial tissue, quickly devour the eyes, and begin to burrow into each person's skull. Once they have feasted on the brain they begin to burrow down the neck into the person's torso and eat each victim from the inside out. Their metabolisms have been heightened due to starvation and adrenaline, and they continuously eat without slowing down. Each person that was attacked has their remaining eyeball roll back into their heads, foam violently from the mouth, and proceed to seizure violently on the floor. Once these rodents have their way with your brain the only thing your body can do is go limp and accept fate. Several people including Hanzel's father died in that mortuary and no one knew who had caused this atrocity.

Present time

Gretel made her way quietly to the door. Before she opens it, she hears slow steps creeping towards the door. She quickly started to feel around the room away from the door. Then she felt something cold and squishy. In a feat of desperation she pulled a damp leather blanket over herself. Suddenly the door swung open and the crazed old woman walked into the room, the light blinding Hanzel who was chained to the wall. "You are going to make a delicious roast, stew, and anything I make out of you." said the crazed old woman. She begins to salivate and starts caressing her own body with her long, boney fingers. "Yes...I am going to love eating your corpse. I just might shove a skewer up your ass, through your body, and out your eye socket." The crazed old lady becomes aroused and pisses on the floor in front of the little boy. "I cannot wait to slice your flesh off as it cooks in my fireplace. Flesh slowly roasting, your hair burns off your body, and you scream until you die from the pain." The crazed old woman said while smacking her lips together and licking her hands as if she were licking sauce off them.

The puddle of urine crept closer to Gretel. The light revealed that the leather blanket wasn't a blanket; it was the skin of a teenage boy the crazed old woman skinned 4 days prior. Dried blood patches covered the skin. The smell of the rotting flesh was making Gretel want to vomit. The smell is gut wrenching and vile. She wanted to vomit but she kept swallowing her own vomit in an attempt to not alert the sick, twisted old woman.

The old crazed old woman hears something in the room. "What is that sound?" The crazed old woman asked Hanzel. "It's my stomach," Hanzel said, "the food you gave me wasn't fresh and my stomach hurts." The crazed old woman slowly smiled with her tongue slowly going across her upper lip. "It's time," said the crazed old woman. "What time? What do you mean?" Hanzel asked in fear. The crazed old woman ignored Hanzel; she walked out of the room, and slammed the door behind her.

The crazed old woman walked down the hall, towards her kitchen, then walked out the front door. She was going to her woodpile to gather wood for her fireplace. She was going to roast Hanzel on a spit.

Hanzel looked at Gretel and said, "You must hurry! Her meal time is quickly approaching." Gretel came out of hiding and projectile vomit all over the floor and wall. "I need to move fast. I cannot take this place anymore." Gretel said. "I will return with the key and we shall get out of here. I promise."

The house was silent and you could hear the woman outside gathering wood. Gretel peered out the door and there was no sign of the crazed old woman. She made a break for the kitchen down the hall, pausing to look around for the crazed old woman. "No sign of her," whispered Gretel. She looked over to the right of the room and there was the book by the stove. Gretel retrieved the book, opened it, and to her horror the key bookmarked the recipe for roast boy on a spit. She quickly grabbed the key and ran to Hanzel. "Quick! Give me your chains!" Gretel exclaimed. As soon as she unlocked the last shackle, it slipped out of her hand and made a loud BOOM on the floor, she placed the key in her pocket, and they began their escape.

They ran for the kitchen and the door handle began to turn. They made a dash for under the table, and they were concealed by a white table cloth covering the table. The table cloth was a clean, never used table cloth. Gretel waved to Hanzel to quickly get under the table and Hanzel obeyed her. Then suddenly, seconds after they make their way under the table, the crazed old woman walks in the house with an arm full of sticks and tinder. She placed all the flammable material in her fireplace, pulled out her homemade spirits and poured some on the dry wood. With her flint and knife she lights a mighty fire in her fireplace. "Now to get the delicious little shit and shove this spit up his ass and begin roasting," said the crazed old woman. She walks towards the room where he was imprisoned, spit in hand, opened the door, and realized he was missing. "Where are you little shit!? I am hungry! Get over here now!" the crazed old woman shrieked. The crazed old woman made her way to the kitchen again and she noticed blood streaks on her clean table cloth. She took aim with the spit and threw it towards the space under the table, and threw it with all her might. The spit cut the skin of Gretel's leg open and she began to bleed. "Owwwww!" exclaimed Gretel, "RUN!"

Suddenly, Hanzel and Gretel burst out from under the table, tipping it over to create a barrier between them and the crazed old woman; Hanzel grabbed the spit and pulled it out of the floor. The crazed old woman became psychotic and blood thirsty. "I am going to kill both you little shits," he crazed old woman growled; "I am going to enjoy slicing your flesh off as you slowly burn to death." The crazed old woman moves the table out of the way, and grinding her teeth so hard blood drips from her mouth, she makes a mad dash at the kids. Hanzel rears back, holds the pointed end towards the crazed old woman, and plunges the spit into the crazed old woman's eye and out the back of her head.

The crazed old woman's life quickly escapes her. Gretel grabbed the cookbook and then the kids charged through the front door, opened it, and ran from the house as fast as they could. With her last dying breaths she utters, "Cursed be Gretel who took my food from me. Curse her that holds the boy's key." The lifeless body of the crazed old woman laid cold and motionless with the spit making its way through the back of her head. The crazed old woman never got her last meal.

The children ran until they got outside the Mystic Forest and then they both collapsed. Both children felt like they had been running forever. Their legs felt like rubber, their feet felt heavy as lead, and slowly coming to realization that they are now safe. Panting heavily they looked at one another and smiled with a sigh of relief. "Do you think she is dead?" asked Hanzel. "Yes, I believe so. No one could have survived that," replied Gretel. "Do you know where we are? I don't recognize this place at all," said Hanzel. "No," Gretel said. "This place is new to me, too." They lay next to each other and stared into the bright sky. Clouds were overhead and full of different shapes and sizes. For hours they just stared at the sky talking, until Hanzel said, "I don't know your name." Gretel looked over and said, "My name is Gretel. What are you called?" Hanzel said, "I am called Hanzel."

They got up, hugged each other, and went to look for building supplies to build a shelter for the night. By nightfall they had built a small log tent for the night. They cuddled up to one another and fell asleep. When day rolled over the countryside they woke up together relieved to still be alive. They had many great conversations and found out they were born in the same year and that they were both only 11-years-old. They forage for berries, sticks, logs, and made spears to catch fish. Life was simply survival and taking care of each other. As the years flew by, they improved their home and lived off the land. They improved on their hunting techniques and foraging each day to make life easier.

Chapter 4 – A Life Together

Surviving off the land for the past 10 years was exhausting and tiresome. One day they were visited by some travelers who also were traders. They were impressed with what they gathered, made in the woods, and in their home that they bestowed them with clothes, pots, pans, guns, ammo, and many other supplies. All Hanzel and Gretel had to do was make art pieces and find various goods in the forest. With clothes and other amenities, they felt like people again.

Since Hanzel and Gretel had been together for 10 years, they decided to join in a sacred union together. They married each other in their own way out in the forest and vowed their undying love for one another. They tried to conceive a child but were not able to. With no doctors nearby they had to keep trying. Along with the trials of conceiving a child, they realized the traders stopped coming around and they never found the reason.

Five years later, Gretel conceived a child and was very happy. She sang to her baby, read to it, and talked to it all the time. But one fateful day, she was out by the creek where she lost her balance and fell into the creek. She landed on a protruding rock by the creeks edge she began to bleed profusely from her vagina. She limped home and Hanzel asked, "What happened? Are you two ok?" Gretel looked at Hanzel and said, "I cannot feel the baby anymore.

Something is wrong baby." A feeling of ice fell over Hanzel's body, he could hardly move. When he came to he saw the blood over Gretel's skirt and began to cry. Days passed and Hanzel never left his wife's side. He fetched her food, water, and any comfort she needed, but the baby was no more. Gretel's stomach began to shrink and flatten out for her body and absorbed the unborn fetus. Devastated, Gretel became very depressed and her soul filled with sorrow. She became distant and cold towards Hanzel. Gretel barely ate or slept for many months due to her increasing depression.

Many months passed and Gretel approached Hanzel and said, "My loving husband. I am so sorry about how I have been towards you. You are a great man and I love you so much. How can I make it up to you?" Hanzel looked at his beautiful bride, smiled, and said, "My beautiful bride. I stayed with you because I never wanted to leave you. You needed me and I vowed to take care of you, no matter the situation." They looked into each other's eyes and shared a very passionate kiss.

That night they lay on the grass just staring into the sky as they did as children; and discussed the night sky, the stars, and their bright future together. They lay side-by-side, holding each other's hands, pulling each other close, and then passionately kiss each other. As the moon brightens the night sky, Hanzel and Gretel begin to undress each other. As they become more aggressive, their arousal begins to explode. Gretel straddles Hanzel's lap, pulls his face into her supple breasts, he begins sucking on her hardened nipples, she grabs Hanzel's hair, and she begins to moan. Gretel's head swings back as she continues to moan loudly and her femininity begins to drench Hanzel's lap. Hanzel caresses Gretel's back, still sucking those beautiful beasts, kisses her neck, then latches on with his teeth. Gretel inhales with pain and severe arousal. Hanzel grabs and begins massaging Gretel's firm ass. "Oh my creator," Gretel screamed, "Eat my pussy! I want to feel you suck on my clit and shove that tongue in my pussy." Hanzel rolled Gretel to her back and ripped her soaked panties off. He lowered his head and began licking her clit gently then descended to her pussy and teased her with light penetrations. Her pussy was glistening with female arousal; so wet she could soak a bed. "Then he raised his head back to her clit, began sucking aggressively, and inserted 3 fingers into her pussy. "Oh my fuck! Oh yes!" Gretel squealed, "Fuck that pussy! I wanna be your whore!" Hanzel pumped his fingers aggressively and continued licking and sucking her clit. "Oh my creator! Harder! I am going to cum!" screamed Gretel, "I am almost there! Keep going!" Hanzel pumped as hard and as fast and he could and Gretel's muscles began to contract and tighten. Her climax was so intense she grabbed her shirt, bit down, screamed with intensity, shot cum from her pussy, and bit through the fabric. "Get on your back!" Gretel commanded, "I am going to make that cock mine!"

Gretel pinned Hanzel to the ground and said, "For being such a real man, I am going to make you feel like a god." She kissed Hanzel's lips, neck, and

asked Gretel seductively. Hanzel replied completely under Gretel's sexual control, "Yes I want that pussy. Oh my creator, I want that fucking pussy. Thrust my hard cock deep in your cunt."

Hanzel turns Gretel over, places her on her back, rubs his cock up and down her pussy, and sticks just the head of his dick into her pussy. Back-and-forth he takes the head of his dick in and out, never fully penetrating her yet. Gretel begins to beg for his cock inside of her, "Fuck me baby. Fuck me hard and deep I want to feel you blow your load inside of my pussy." Hanzel takes control of Gretel's body and he looks deep into Gretel's eyes, "I will make a woman out of you, if it's the last thing I do. Hanzel grabs a hold of his cock, wets it with Gretel's pussy juices, and then rams his cock deep as he possibly can into her pussy. Gretel moans with excitement as she begs for more, more, and more. Gretel continues to moan passionately begging for Hanzel to fuck her harder. Hanzel begins to thrust his dick slow to get his rhythm going. And then he begins to thrust harder with every thrust. "Oh my creator," screamed Gretel, "you feel so good deep inside of my pussy. I can hear how wet I am." Gretel's pussy and Hanzel's cock are glistening from the hot passionate sex. Both begin to breathe heavier with each thrust from Hanzel's mighty cock.

Both Hanzel and Gretel sweat profusely, their bodies dripping sweat from all over their bodies. As both of them climax, Hanzel's body begins to contract, every muscle in his body tightens up and he unleashes his ejaculate inside of Gretel's wet pussy. Hanzel's cock pulsates violently as he unleashes his baby milk and juice inside of Gretel's pussy. Gretel screams as her body lightly spasms as she climaxes, her eyes are in the back of her head, and she comes all over Hanzel's cock. Both barely able to breathe and extremely winded from the passion and embrace they had shared for untold amounts of time.

Hanzel leans in and kisses Gretel very passionately on her lips. Gretel wraps her arms around his neck and draws them in as they lock lips. Their eyes are closed, tongues wrestling, and their hearts racing. They run their fingers through each other's hair as they continue to kiss passionately rolling around in the grass.

Both exhausted from the hot and steamy sex they lay looking at the stars. Hanzel and Gretel lay next to each other in the grass cuddled up under the stars. Neither one of them could believe the intensity of their sexual embrace. Panting heavily and sweating profusely even after they had concluded. They did nothing except look into each other's eyes and they knew their love had never been stronger. Hanzel pulls Gretel in close, puts her head on his chest, and firmly hugs her and holds her head gingerly on his chest. Gretel looks up, moves her hand passed Hanzel's ear, and she passionately kisses him. After that kiss, they vowed to never let anything like a miscarriage come between them.

Chapter 5 – Meal of Life

Many decades pass into the golden years of Hanzel and Gretel. Life couldn't be sweeter for these two love birds. Their love had never been stronger and nothing could come between them. Hanzel and Gretel have experienced much and have made many friends throughout the years. They have met many travelers and traders that have come through and done many transactions. Hanzel and Gretel have done so many transactions; they have flourished their cottage into a small homestead. They now raise various animals including a pig, a goose, a horse, a cow, and a friendly fox that has become part of the family. They have continuous ammunition for the rifle Hanzel acquired and other tools for harvesting. Life is simple, quiet, and nothing could make it better.

One bright sunny morning, Hanzel and Gretel were sitting in their favorite chairs. Hanzel was cleaning his rifle and Gretel was reading her favorite book. Hanzel was preparing for a hunt but couldn't decide on what to bring home for dinner. "Honey?" asked Hanzel, "What would you like to eat this evening? You let me choose the last few meals, what is your desire?" Gretel thought, "Well I would love to have a duck dinner but there hasn't been any around. Maybe wild pig? Yes, wild pig." Gretel then spoke up, "My darling husband, bring a wild pig home. I'll cook up a feast for us. After all, we deserve a banquet after the wonderful year we had," Hanzel stood up and said, "You know we haven't had wild pig in a while. They have been scarce lately, but I shall bring you home a pig my love. You always have the best ideas." Hanzel bent down and kissed Gretel on the lips. "Thank you, honey. I'll have a special surprise for you upon your return." Hanzel slung his rifle over his right shoulder and said, "You are too good for me. I do not deserve you." Gretel replied, "Oh go on you. You are too much. But I love you too. They kissed one another and Hanzel disappeared into the Mystic Forest to bring back a wild pig.

As Hanzel disappears into the Mystic Forest, he begins to plan his trip on finding a wild pig. He remembered that there was a family of wild pigs due northwest of the house about a 6 hour walk. He took a deep breath and went on his way. This journey is going to be dangerous but worth it once he sees his wife's eye light up.

Gretel went to the kitchen and began to prepare her surprise for Hanzel. She looked around for her cookbook and couldn't find it. But under the counter she spotted the cookbook she took from the crazed old woman when she was a child. "Maybe there is a decent pastry recipe in this book. After all, it is only a cookbook." As she scanned the recipes one by one, she saw horrific images that only brought up the horrible parts of her past with that sick old woman. At last she came across a ginger bread recipe and she read over the ingredients. "I have all these ingredients, except the black ginger root. This root is found in the flats of the Mystic Forest by the Pine

Grove. "That is about an hour's walk from here." She thought. "But Hanzel is searching for a pig that we haven't seen in months." So Gretel began gathering ingredients out of the garden, got water out of the well, placed those items in the kitchen, and then went on a search for the black ginger root.

Gretel set out into the Mystic Forest to find the black ginger root. About an hour into her search she came upon the Pine Grove and she began looking for the ginger root. Then after a few short minutes of scavenging she came across a large patch of black ginger root. "I'll take a few back just in case so I can have some for a later time." She thought. During her trip back home she came across a large black berry bush. Being that she had been walking for some time she decided to stop a while and have a light snack. She gathered a couple handfuls of berries, sat by the bush, and relaxed. She watched the little woodland creatures run across the forest floor and through the trees. "I never realized how beautiful this place is," Gretel thought to herself, "I should bring Hanzel here for a picnic." She felt warm inside just thinking of the romantic day they could have just sitting in the Pine Grove. So after she had eaten some berries, she gathered a few for her husband, and she continued on home.

During her walk home she noticed that her skin was getting dry and flakey. "Why do I feel dry? I hope I am not having a reaction to anything." Gretel thought might be just from the journey. So she continued on home and began humming a happy tune. Suddenly she hears the sound of a lone wolf attacking a pig. It sounded like a brutal attack. "I better move quickly," Gretel whispered to herself, "there may be more wolves on the way." The sound appeared to be carrying for a long distance but Gretel didn't want to leave anything to chance.

Soon Gretel arrived at home at around noon. Now time to create my ginger pastry. Gretel's feet were sore from the journey but she was determined to give her husband a delicious pastry for dessert. She laid out all the ingredients and began to mix them together. She peered at the recipe at the bottom of the page and it read "The black ginger root, is a powerful root for it is…….." the rest is smeared and illegible. Gretel shrugged her shoulders and thought "it must be potent in taste" and continued on with the recipe. Once the dough reached the right texture and consistency she rolled it out into a flat sheet. "Hmmmm. Should I make this into a loaf of gingerbread? A house?" Gretel talked out loud to herself. "Not enough time for a loaf or a house. Plus I don't want to trigger my husband. He endured so much when we escaped." Her throat became scratchy all of a sudden. "Oh my I hope I am not getting sick. I'll use the peppermint, green tea, and honey to take care of that." Gretel got her favorite tea pot out and brewed herself some soothing tea to prevent her illness.

While she waited for her water to boil, Gretel continued with her creation. "You know what I will shape it like a man and decorate it for Hanzel, " said

Gretel, "Oh my, he will love it. I haven't done anything like that in years." With much excitement, she began carefully shaping the gingerbread man with her knife. With much precision and focus she completed cutting out the gingerbread man shape. She carefully picked up the gingerbread man and placed it on a cooking sheet and baked the pastry. She had leftover dough and decided to put it away for a later time.

Gretel heard her teapot beginning to whistle and she grabbed her favorite cup so she may enjoy the tea she had been waiting for. Gretel poured herself a nice cup of tea, added a bit of honey to it, and took a little sip. "Oh my creator," said Gretel, "this is just what I needed." Gretel went to her favorite chair and sat down and began reading her book while she waited for the gingerbread man to finish baking. This book brings back many good memories for her and she never gets tired of reading it. Her favorite book is an adventure book. It tells the tale of a young man who saves a princess from a dreaded fate in a tower worse than death. Gretel always wondered if things like that ever really happened in real life, but she will never know.

When the gingerbread man was finished baking, Gretel removed the sheet from the oven and set it on the counter to cool. She prepared icing and little candies to decorate the gingerbread man. "White icing, gum drop buttons, and candy coated chocolate buttons. I knew these would be used very soon," thought Gretel, "I am so glad I bought these from those travelers last week." As soon as the gingerbread man was cool enough, Gretel began to decorate. Gave him a white belt, white cuffs, white shoes, 3 gumdrop buttons, shirt outline, 2 chocolate buttons for eyes and nose, and a smile she designed with her knife. She picked up the dessert then placed it on the oven.

Gretel turned around to begin cleaning up her utensils and mixing bowls. When she turned around the gingerbread man was missing. She could hear scurrying little feet across the floor. "Who is there?" asked Gretel, "what do you want? Where is my gingerbread man that I made for my husband?" Gretel grabs the knife that she used to carve the gingerbread man's mouth and holds it close to her body trying to conceal it. Gretel searches her kitchen then suddenly hears the scurrying going across your floor again. "Show yourself, do you hear me, show yourself now!" The scurrying continues with little pitter patter of very small feet on the floor. "Oh no," said Gretel, "I hope I do not have mice or rats. I hate mice and rats."

As Gretel turns around and looks at the floor she sees a dark shadowy figure peering out from behind her counter. "I can see you," exclaimed Gretel, "I can see you peering from beyond my counter. What did you do with my gingerbread man? That was for my husband." The shadowy figure that is no bigger than half a baking sheet moved its head side to side appearing to try to comprehend what she is saying to them. The shadowy figure appeared to be hesitant coming out of hiding. It would begin to walk out but would quickly go behind the counter and peer out at Gretel again. Gretel started to walk towards the shadowy figure slowly and the shadowy figure began to make a hissing sound. Like a very angry snake ready to strike its attacker, "Hissssssssssssss!" the shadowy figure sounded, as Gretel continues to creep closer to the shadowy figure. Suddenly it growls at her, signaling to back off, for she got too close. Gretel quickly backed off for she became very scared. Her heart was racing in her chest and fear that she was about to be attacked, maimed, or possibly killed by this thing. The shadowy figure continues to tilt its head back and forth studying Gretel's every facial movement and her other physical movements. "It's okay, I'm sorry for being so angry earlier," said Gretel, "you startled me. Can you come out so I can see you?" Then suddenly Gretel heard, "come… out?" Puzzled Gretel looked at the shadowy figure and asked, "What did you say?" The shadowy figure again asked, "come… out?" Gretel was very intrigued by this new development. She thought to herself 'how can I make this thing come out so I can see it?'

With her next effort, Gretel held out her arms inviting the shadowy figure to come out to receive a hug. Soon the shadowy figure stepped out into the light, looked at Gretel, and began to study her. Gretel was shocked to see her gingerbread man was alive. Her heart was racing not knowing what to expect with this encounter. "Who are you, if I may ask?" asked Gretel, "Where did you come from?" The gingerbread man just squinted and tried to mimic what he just saw. Gretel was amazed that this thing was learning so fast. As she continued to talk to him, the gingerbread man began to start speaking. He quickly learned speech, gestures, body language, etc. It was like he was playing catch up.

Within a few hours the gingerbread man could speak full sentences and use body language. The gingerbread man asked, "What can I call you?" Gretel was confused and she thought hard. She thought that since she created him and she had no children she replied, "You can call me 'Momma'. I'll be your momma." Suddenly the gingerbread man smiled and felt something he had never felt before, love. "Momma, what am I called?" asked the gingerbread man, "can I have a name?" Gretel took a moment to think. "I never even picked out a name for the child we lost years ago," she thought, "what to name him, what to name him." Then the name was obvious to her. "Well sweetheart, I will call you Ginger," said Gretel. With much excitement and enthusiasm Ginger jumped up and down and danced all over the room. "Yay! I am called Ginger," exclaimed Ginger, "I have a name!"

After many attempts to get Ginger's attention, Ginger looks at Gretel and asks, "Ginger, do you know where you came from or who you were?" Ginger looked at her and said, "Yes, mommy. I do." Gretel asked, "Who were you and where did you come from?" Ginger said, "I am the baby that was lost years ago. I was given a second chance. I remember on the other side, someone said the root you used to make my body was magical." "Who said that?" asked Gretel, "Who said the root was magical?" Ginger just shrugged and said, "I don't know, I couldn't see him in the darkness. He did say I was getting a second chance but it was not going to be easy."

Gretel began to tear up and she reached out for Ginger, inviting him in for a hug. Ginger reached in acceptance of her hug and stepped towards her. Gretel picked Ginger up and the shared the most heartfelt and warmest hug both ever experienced. "I never felt such love before in my life," said Gretel, "despite the situation, you are my baby boy." Ginger hugged Gretel tightly and didn't want to let go.

Gretel smelled the air and the smell of gingerbread was mouthwatering. Unknowingly, Gretel attempted to eat Ginger. "Mommy!" exclaimed Ginger, "What are you doing?" Gretel snapped out of it and said, "Oh my creator, I am so sorry. Please forgive me." Ginger just smiled and remembered he has a pastry for a body. "It is ok mommy, I understand that I smell delicious," laughed Ginger, "I would eat me too if I could." Gretel was a little uneasy about Ginger's statement. But she realized right away that he was reincarnated today and didn't understand his words.

Gretel set Ginger down on the floor and told him to go play. Ginger runs outside and begins to frolic around the yard. He admires the sky, the grass, the trees, the air, and begins to explore. "Wow! This feels very nice," said Ginger, "this is so amazing. I cannot believe what I see and feel right now." Ginger begins to roll around in the grass, pick dandelions, and throw them in the air. Ginger could hardly contain himself with all this new stuff that he is experiencing. He felt very proud to be alive and to have such a wonderful momma. "I cannot believe all these things around me," said Ginger, "I wonder if momma has seen all this before." Ginger ran inside the house full of excitement and asked Gretel, "mommy have you seen all that stuff outside? It is beautiful and I can't believe my eyes." Gretel smiled and remembered that he just came to life today. "Yes my dear," said Gretel, "there are many beautiful things in this world, and I hope you get to see all of it. Now run along and go play on the yard." Ginger giggled the cutest little laugh and ran back outside with excitement.

Chapter 6 – The Unfamiliar

Ginger walked around the yard and he suddenly felt discomfort in his stomach. "What am I feeling? It's uncomfortable with my second button? I am scared. I better talk to momma." He ran into the cottage, into the kitchen and said, "Momma, it hurts by my second button. What should I do?" Puzzled, Gretel looked at Ginger and asked, "Pardon? You have pain by your second button?" Ginger replied, "Yes momma," he pointed at his stomach region, "It hurts right here." Gretel smiled and said, "Oh my dear. No need to worry. You are just hungry." Confused and worried Ginger asked, "What is 'hungry'? I do not understand." Gretel picked up Ginger and smiled again, "When you are 'hungry', your body is telling you to eat." Gretel set Ginger on the counter, picked up an apple she harvested that morning, took a bite, and demonstrated how to eat food.

"This is strange," Ginger thought, "But if it will take away the pain, I will try it." So Ginger asked Gretel, "Can I try Momma?" Gretel said, "Of course honey. I want you to not feel that way. Here try this apple." Gretel handed the apple to Ginger; Ginger opened his mouth, took a small bite, and then chewed as Gretel taught him. Gretel stopped smiling suddenly when she realized that Ginger had no teeth. "My sweet boy, how are you able to bite and chew? You don't have any teeth." Ginger shrugged his shoulders and continued to eat the apple. When he finished the apple Gretel said, "Honey, please open your mouth."

Ginger complied with his mother's request. Visually there is no sign of teeth. "What in the world? How can he bite into that apple?" She placed her finger on Ginger's lower jaw, ran it across the outer rim, and she left a trail of blood on his lip." Shocked, she said, "Oh my creator! What the hell? How did you do that?" Ginger curled into a nervous ball and was shaking. "Sorry momma, I didn't mean to. Please don't stop loving me." Gretel picked Ginger up and gave him a hug, "I could never stop loving you, my baby boy. It was an accident and you had no idea. I will never stop loving you." Ginger smiled and said, "I love you momma. Can I help you with your cut?" Gretel smiled and said, "Of course, let me go get the bandages." Ginger smacked his lips together and thought that was tasty.

As Gretel brought the bandages over to Ginger, Ginger slurped the remaining blood off his lips into his mouth and swallowed. "How can I help, momma?" asked Ginger in a sweet voice. "Hold this jar of tree sap for me while I prepare the bandages," said Gretel. With much pride, Ginger held the jar for his momma. Ginger observed Gretel bandaging up her finger but what he was really after is the blood in which he sampled before. "That was delicious," Ginger thought, "I want more. The taste, the feel of it in my mouth, and the warmth; I must have more!" Ginger thought to himself, "No! I cannot keep drinking mommy. She loves me."

"Sap please," said Gretel, "I need it to keep the bandage in place." Ginger pushed the jar of sap to

Gretel with a smile on his face. "I feel important," he thought to himself, "I want mommy to be better." Gretel used an old knife to dip into the sap and spread it on the bandage flap. "Just a little amount will do or else you make a mess." Gretel told Ginger. "Hehe," Ginger giggled, "If you make a mess mommy, I will help you clean it up." With one final press down on the bandage, Gretel's finger was bandaged. "Thank you, sweet heart. You were very helpful," said Gretel. "Thank you for showing me mommy," replied Ginger. Ginger had watched the whole process from start to finish. He felt very important.

Gretel grabbed the bandages and Ginger put the lid back on the sap jar. "Here you go mommy," said Ginger, "I did this for you." Gretel tested the top and it was nice and snug. "Nicely done my little helper," said Gretel, "Glad you could help me get better." Ginger smiled and asked for more food to eat. "Oh my goodness, I forgot to make you more food," said Gretel, "how about a nice sandwich." Ginger looked confused because he had no idea what a sandwich was. Gretel cut off 2 slices of bread placed, them on a plate, and found the salami she got from a traveler not more than 3 days ago. She cut a couple slices off the salami, placed them on the bread, and sectioned the sandwich into 4 sections. "Try this, it is a salami sandwich," said Gretel, "it is yummy." Ginger picked up a section of the sandwich and took a bite. He liked the taste but didn't love it. "Can I have some of that red stuff from your finger on this sandwich?" asked Ginger. Horrified, Gretel said, "No, absolutely not, that is disgusting! I am sorry my dear, but that isn't ok." Ginger shrugged his shoulders and simply replied, "Ok," and ate the rest of the sandwich.

Gretel turned around and she noticed a large dry patch of skin on her arm. She scratched it for a moment and felt it tear but no blood. "That is strange," she thought, "what is going on with my skin?" Ginger noticed Gretel rubbing her arm. "Mommy," he said, "are you ok?" Gretel turned around, smiled, and replied, "Yes sweetheart. I am fine. Why don't you go play outside for a while? It's a sunny day out. Plus if you are hungry try some fruits and vegetables in the garden." Ginger smiled and said, "Ok mommy, I will go play. I found an interesting rock earlier, wanna see it later?" "Yes sweetheart," said Gretel, "I would love that." Ginger ran out the door screaming, "YAAAAAAAAAAAAAAAAAAAAAAAAAAAAAY YYYYY!"

Ginger ran through the yard and rolled around in the grass. He was so happy to be alive. Ginger went behind the house were Hanzel and Gretel's garden is located. The garden was full of strawberries, blackberries, lettuce, carrots, cabbage, squash, and many more items to eat. Ginger was just amazed at all the plants and how beautiful everything was. He tried a bit of everything and began snacking on a few fruits and vegetables. He enjoyed the flavor and the smells of the garden. His favorite smell of all was the flowers planted around the whole garden, except one entrance path by the house. "Those things were tasty but not as tasty as the red stuff that came from mommy's finger," Ginger thought to himself, "it was so warm and delicious. I hope I can have more soon."

A thought came over Ginger suddenly, "Where's my daddy?" Ginger ran inside the house and asked Gretel, "Mommy, where is my daddy?" Gretel stopped cleaning the kitchen and said, "He is out hunting for a wild pig for us. He might be a while since we haven't seen any wild pigs for some time now." Ginger felt a bit of sadness, "But he will return, right?" Gretel looked over and said, "Yes your father has taken on many things in the wild, and he will return before we know it." Ginger smiled and said, "Ok mommy." Then Ginger went back outside to play.

Chapter 7 – The Torment Begins

Off to the west, there is a pasture with a river down in the valley and a few trees spaced out randomly. Around the 10 acre pasture perimeter is a wooden fence holding in a few animals Hanzel and Gretel accumulated over the years. They have a goose, a pig, a cow, a horse, and a fox that roamed about the property. All five were staring at Ginger and salivating profusely. "Get over here little morsel!" said the Goose. "I am going to enjoy eating you," said the pig. "I will eat you slowly and enjoy each bite," said the cow. "You will never get away from me. I am faster than you," said the horse. "I'll figure your every move and when you least expect it, I will bite off your head and rape your corpse, then finish the rest of you," said the fox with a pulsing erection.

Frightened, Ginger started to run for the house and the fox, horse, and cow leapt over the fence after him. "Get back here!" demanded the fox, "I am throbbing to taste your flesh!" The horse yelled, "Get your crunchy goodness back here!" The cow yelled, "I will enjoy you with a bit of my own milk." The goose had taken flight and tried to fly after ginger, "Flight is faster than you. I will have you all to myself." The pig stayed behind the fence and laughed to himself, "those fools will never catch him in time." Ginger got into the house and slammed the door shut. The fox, the horse, and the cow stopped just feet from the door. The goose didn't maneuver fast enough and went head first into the door and broke his neck. The goose was still alive but in excruciating pain. "Dammit Goose," said the fox, "you almost landed on me you dumbass." The goose's body continues to twitch and spasm. "Horse," the cow said, "mercy kill." The horse nodded in approval, reared back, and with a mighty blow with his powerful front hooves, crushed the goose's head and decapitated all in one blow. Blood and body matter were sprayed all over the front door and front step. The horse stepped back and said, "Well that's done. Hope he went to a better place than here. Come on; let's go back to the pasture." So the cow, the horse, and the fox returned to the pasture."

Before the goose became a goose, he was an elegant man who enjoyed the fine arts and cuisine. His name is unknown to this day but nobody cared when he disappeared. Nothing could be better for the man who became a goose then to go see a play, an opera, or even a ballet. This man was also very rude and conceited. He thought that just because he was cultured and witty that he could treat people with disrespect and disdain. After the last ballet he saw he went to the local market to pick up some food for the evening because he was expecting female company. Many people took notice of his conceited nature in the marketplace and grew to hate him very quickly. "These vegetables are rotten and I will not purchase this array of vile harvest." He continued through the market and tried to find the most impressive ingredients for his meal tonight. He came across a stand full of fruits and vegetables that have never been seen before. He looked at the shopkeeper and asked, "Are these fresh today? For you see I am cooking a goose that I'd killed earlier this morning. And I have my lovely woman coming to feast with me tonight." The shopkeeper looked at the man and said, "Why yes sir, all my fruits and vegetables are picked the same day I sell them. Anything in particular you are looking for?" The man looked at the shopkeeper and asked, "What would you recommend for a wild goose?" The shopkeeper had been watching this man for quite some time walking in the marketplace. And thought this man should learn some manners. "I'll tell you what sir I will share my most honored secret with you," said the shopkeeper, "This is ground ginger root and it will give your goose the perfect flavor." The man had been cooking for quite some time and he was puzzled to realize, or to be told, that ginger root would go great with wild goose. "Really? This will give it the perfect flavor?" The shopkeeper looked at him with a grin, "yes sir. This'll be a meal you never forget." The man looked at the shopkeeper and asked, "Why is it black?" The shopkeeper looked at him and said, "I can tell you are a man of fancy and rare items. This is a rare root called 'black ginger root' and it is a rare root with a fabulous taste. Very few people know where to find this root and I am one of a small handful. Trust me when I say this meal will be one you'll never forget." Intrigued, the man paid the shopkeeper with a smile, "thank you good sir. If all goes well tonight I will reward you generously." The shopkeeper replied, "No gratitude necessary sir, you just enjoy your evening and that will be thank you enough." Both men said their goodbyes and the man was on his way home.

The man made his way home to begin preparing his meal for his lady visitor. The man stopped for a moment during his travels home and pulled out the ground up ginger root. He took a moment to try and see how this particular spice was going to make his goose unforgettable. He licked the tip of his right pointer finger, put it onto the powdered ginger root, and dabbed it on his tongue. The man thought to himself, "Hmmmm, this is actually pretty good. I'll have to stop back tomorrow and pay that man handsomely. I would've never thought that black ginger root would have gone so well with my bird."

As the man was just feet from his front door he began to feel odd. He began to become very dizzy, disoriented, and could no longer keep his balance. And before that man knew what was happening he had blacked out in front of his house. People passing by his house never stopped to help him because they knew who he was and what kind of a man he was. The next day the man woke up and felt very strange. When he went to rub his head, he couldn't feel his head. He looked at his hands and realized that his hands were gone. All he could see were feathers on what he could see were wings and not arms. When he looked at his nose, he no longer had a nose. He had a beak, one of a goose. Strangely enough he knew how to fly with his new wings as if he had been doing it for years. He began flapping his wings and looked inside of his house only to find that his body was laying on his countertop with a shotgun blast to the face. "What happened to me? Why am I dead on my countertop but I still live," asked the-now-goose, "I am dead and naked on my own countertop. What the hell happened?" Confusion wafted over the goose and fear began to course through his veins. "Why is this happening to me? This is impossible because I do not do magic tricks. That cannot be my dead body on that table with half my face blown off."

What the man had not realized is he had been unconscious for days. The people that passed them by knew what had happened to him and they didn't care what happened to the man. Over those days he slowly transformed into the goose that he had killed but switched roles. Meaning he went from a live human to an alive goose while the dead goose became a dead human. The now-goose took flight to find the man who gave him the black ginger root but was unable to locate him. Everyone he tried to talk to, tried to kill him because it's not murder if you try to kill a goose especially if you're going to eat them. Then out of nowhere a net went around the goose and his wings were instantly clipped so he could not fly very well. "You have finally found me my friend, but what you don't know is you're going for a little ride," said the shopkeeper, "now to give you something to help you relax for a little trip." Before the goose could say anything he had a rake with a very powerful smelling fluid on it over his beak and he was unconscious again. The next thing he knew he was being unloaded off the wagon with a cow, horse, and a pig. The goose had no recollection of what had happened or transpired the past few days. All he knew is this was going to be his new home from now on, and never knew what his future beheld him.

The front door cracked open slowly, and Ginger reached for the goose's corpse. Once he grabbed hold of the goose's lifeless body, he dragged it quickly into the house. Ginger closed the door and began to consume the raw dead body of the goose. Starting at the crushed head, he began to bite off large sections of the goose's head including the beak. The crunching of the skull begins to excite Ginger. The taste, the texture, and the sheer thrill of this delicious dead animal made him want MORE. He swallows the remainder of the goose's head and begins to munch on the goose's neck like it was a banana. But first, Ginger pins the goose's neck down with his feet, pinches the base of the neck by the goose's shoulders, and milks the remaining blood out of the goose's neck. He sees a different colored liquid coming out of the spinal cord. Ginger latches on to the spinal cord and siphons out the spinal fluid. "MMMMMM, so good." Bite by bite, Ginger was enjoying his unexpected feast. "MMMMMM," he thought, "this is so good and has a delicious crunch to it too." Now Ginger is going to enjoy the main course of his meal, the goose's body. Without removing the feathers or feet, ginger takes chunk after chunk of flesh out of the goose's lifeless corpse.

Ginger looked inside the open cavity of where the goose's neck used to be and saw more delicious treats inside. "Oh my creator, what is that?" Ginger reaches into the goose's body and begins pulling out the goose's internal organs. The slimy, bloody organs pulled out one by one like cookies in a jar, and Ginger is consuming them as he pulls them out. Soon after eating the fresh, raw organs of the goose, Ginger finishes the rest of the goose. Ginger also consumes the remaining feathers and drinks the blood off the floor to make it spotless for his momma.

Gretel watched the whole ordeal and thought, "That is terrifying, but my boy has to eat." With a few deep breaths, and mentally preparing herself, she decides to talk to Ginger. "Hi sweetheart, did you enjoy the goose?" Ginger turned around and said, "Yes mommy, the goose was delicious. But I am still hungry." Puzzled, Gretel looked at Ginger like he just spoke a whole new language to her. "You…are still hungry? Where did all that goose go that you just ate?" asked Gretel. Ginger pointed at his mouth and replied, "In here mommy. I still feel hungry, but I'll be ok for the rest of the day."

The day was getting late and Gretel was getting tired. Ginger was rubbing his eyes and yawning. "Momma I am feeling strange," said Ginger, "I don't feel right and I keep doing something with my mouth." Gretel replied with a smile, "Oh my sweet child, you are tired. Let me make you a bed. With Ginger being no bigger than half a cookie sheet, it was pretty easy to make him a bed. So Gretel looked for a spare pillow and pillow case. She suddenly remembered that she had a spare pillow on the bed with a pillow case. Gretel placed the pillow in an old wooden crate and used the pillow case as a sleeping bag for Ginger. "Here you go my darling," said Gretel with much delight, "a bed for you." Ginger felt so much pride that he got his own bed. "Thank you mommy," he exclaimed, "I am so happy.

I can sleep on this tonight?" Gretel looked at Ginger and said, "Yes, you can sleep on this every night and even when you need to nap in the afternoons." Gretel tucked Ginger in, sang him a lullaby and kissed him goodnight. "I love you Ginger," said Gretel. "I love you more mommy," said Ginger.

Gretel walked back into the kitchen and wondered where Hanzel was. She peered out the window and wondered where Hanzel was; for he had been gone all day. She walked out of the front door and sat on the porch just wondering where he was. Gretel was getting worried because she was still losing skin and starting to lose her teeth. "Hanzel, I need you more than ever. Please come home, we have our son," Gretel said into the night sky.

Chapter 8 – The Pig's Day

It is a bright, cheerful morning and ginger was waking up as the sun kissed his face. "Good morning mommy!" Ginger exclaimed, "The sun is out and I hear birdies. Can I go out to play?" Barely awake Gretel said, "Yes dear. Please go play. Mommy feels ill." Ginger wasn't worried because he wanted his mommy to feel better. "I'll go fetch some berries from the garden for you," Ginger said eagerly, "Would you like that mommy?" Gretel thought what a wonderful child she has. "Yes honey," said Gretel, "maybe you can pick some flowers of your choice and put them in the vase by my bed." Ginger leapt out his bed to the floor and ran to the garden. Gretel noticed a lot of skin flakes all over the bed but she was too tired to care and fell back to sleep.

Ginger began harvesting the flowers first because he wanted to help make his mommy smile. Ginger smelled lavender and that helped him feel calm and relaxed. He thought, "This perfect flower will help mommy relax." So he grabbed as much as he could carry and ran into Gretel's room, where she was fast asleep, and placed the flowers in the vase. Ginger scampered back outside where he saw a few lilac bushes. "Hmmm, I like the pink with the purple flowers," Ginger thought to himself. He grabbed as much as he could carry and ran back into the house. He got up to the vase and placed the lilacs in with the lavender and arranged them in the prettiest way he could. "There," Ginger thought, "mommy will be relaxed and happy to see these."

Ginger thought, "I will go gather some berries for mommy's tummy because she might just be hungry." So he saw a small bowl already next to the bed and decided to fill that bowl with berries. Making many trips to the garden he finally filled that bowl with strawberries, blackberries, and blueberries. "This will help mommy for sure," Ginger said with pride, "Now I will go play for a bit." Ginger scampered out of the house into the yard where he ran around in the grass laughing and giggling.

Ginger noticed that the pig was grazing in the pasture eating any fruit found above ground and vegetables he could find that were buried in the dirt. But Ginger did not know anything about this pig or what he is capable of. For this pig is no ordinary pig; he was once a very powerful man of wealth, riches, and selfishness. This pig was once a man by the name of Harold Hoggbottom, the richest man in a far-off land far from the Mystic Forest. He would show off his wealth and power daily.

Hoggbottom is a psychotic businessman with two types of employees: laborers and slaves. The laborers are paid and free people and the slaves are unpaid and treated terribly. One of his labors in fact had slaves of his choice if he so wished. Hoggbottom gave his laborer the go-ahead to do whatever he pleased with the slaves, because he did not care what happened to the slaves, for he could always just get more.

Hoggbottom would buy women, land, property, etc. just because he could, even if he didn't need to. He liked to eat because he was not a skinny man by any means. In fact, he was well over 450 pounds of gluttonous blubber and loved to eat and waste food. When the poor would come to Hoggbottom asking for money or food, he would physically harm them. By physically harming them we mean anything from a slap across the face to brutally murdering them and having his cook make them into a delicacy. He did not care about human life whatsoever as long as he had what he wanted when he wanted it. In fact, the women he bought were damned to a lifetime of servitude both physical labor and sexual abuse. Hoggbottom's house is massive; his is large enough to fix the entire village inside of that house. Hoggbottom did not care because all the women he had enslaved inside the house. They are all given a strict itinerary of work to do and anytime nothing was done to his satisfaction they were abused in whatever fashion he deemed appropriate, in this means, that they can be killed and made into food for this fat bastard. And sometimes he didn't even bother to cook them; he would eat them raw, and in many cases still alive. Hoggbottom would have them tied down onto the table and he would begin feasting wherever he felt appropriate. Many times he would molest his victims while he bit into their flesh. There were no boundaries when it came to punishment with this fucker.

Hoggbottom's greed and his villainy would be his undoing. For one of the women he bought early in the week was a practitioner in the dark magic realm.

She knew what Hoggbottom was about; for the dark spirits of the dark realm have told her his ways, and they wanted him. They offered to lift her curse if they brought him to justice. So she allowed herself to be purchased by this gluttonous freak of a man so she could get close. For weeks she devised a plan to get close to him, so she could administer her curse upon his being. Using her seductive nature, she lured him into a false sense of security and offered herself sexually in any way he wished. Anything he wanted he could have without question. Hoggbottom, without any suspicion, agreed and grew very aroused and demanded it take place right away.

They went to Hoggbottom's bedchamber and she began to do a seductive dance for him. Unaware of what is being presented to him, the woman was actually in the middle of casting her curse upon him. Too busy to realize what was happening to him, Hoggbottom just began to stroke his penis with excitement. The woman scratched him in intricate, but planned spots in order to make her curse complete. With one final slash across his chest, the woman spoke the words, "for your murder and greed, these words must be heed. Forever cursed for being mankind's smog; I condemn you to be forever all hog." Hoggbottom very quickly started to feel extreme pain in his chest and all the scratches over his body. His body was painfully transforming into a hog and he stayed conscious through the whole transformation. The transformation took hours and the woman stood by and watched while eating an apple and other delectable items. She then summoned all the slave women to witness their freedom coming to fruition. All the women watched and smiled and began to gather items to inflict pain upon him including the whips and chains he used on them.

The transformation is complete and the women began to brutally beat him to unconsciousness. One of the women who received the worst punishments and enslaved the longest, drew a knife from her waistband, and posed to strike him through the heart. But the woman who administered the curse stopped her and said, "Stop! For my friends in the dark realm have informed me there is a fate worse than death waiting for him. Death right now would be too good for him." Then with one swift hit with a club that was next to the bed, the strongest slave woman rendered the pig Hoggbottom unconscious. The next thing he knew he was being unloaded off the wagon with the goose, a cow, and a horse.

Present Day

Ginger noticed the pig had found a way out of the pasture and was about to enter the garden. Ginger looked around when he heard some rustling and he saw the pig. Before he was noticed, Ginger ran for the tool shed by the garden and closed the door behind him. The pig smelled ginger bread and began sniffing out the source of the smell. As the pig tracked Ginger, Ginger climbed on to the bench and began to look for something to defend himself. Suddenly he saw a hatchet and picked it up. "This will have to do," thought Ginger, "I don't know what else to do."

As the sounds of grunting and snorting got closer, Ginger lowered himself just enough to be out of sight. Suddenly the door slowly opens and the pig continues to grunt, snort, and sniff out the smell of gingerbread. "I know you're here little man," said the pig, "I promise this will be quick." Ginger was cornered and scared. "Come out and play with the pretty piggy," said the pig, trying to sound cute and harmless, "we can play games together. All you have to do is jump into my mouth." The pig rears up and places his hooves on the bench. "There you are my little friend," said the pig, "now get into my mouth so this can be quick."

A surge of rage exploded in Ginger's body and he swung the hatchet, splitting the pig's nose, upper and lower jaw in two. The pig jerked back, landed on his back, and the pig was pinned between the shed door and the door frame on his back. The more he struggled, the tighter it got. The pig tried to beg for mercy but all he could do was squeal. Ginger grabbed the hatchet, leapt down from the bench onto the pig's stomach, and demanded in a deep demonic voice, "SHUT THE FUCK UP! YOU'LL WAKE MOMMA!" Ginger began hacking off the pigs legs and the pig squealed even louder. The pig squealed, "You psychotic little cunt! What the fuck is wrong with you?!" Ginger noticed a movement in the pig's throat every time he squealed. Ginger's eyes turned blood red, he took aim, and plunged the hatchet across the pig's throat, instantly silencing the pig, and blood began to spray everywhere. Ginger focused on the blood, he concentrated the blood into a swirling vortex, and the blood flowed like a swirling arch from the pig's throat into Ginger's mouth. Ginger drained the pig of all his blood and when he snapped out of his demonic trance, he was confused. "What just happened?" Ginger thought to himself, "Do I have magic?" Without any further thought, Ginger began to feast on the decapitated legs of the pig. "Yummy," Ginger thought, "I like pig." After finishing with all four of the pig's legs, Ginger removed the embedded hatchet from the pig's throat. Ginger took the blade of the hatchet and ran it from the pig's sternum, through the groin, and hacked away at the rib cage exposing the pig's innards. Like the goose before him, the pig was going to be eaten by a little gingerbread man. Munching away at the pig's internal organs, Ginger was feeling a thrill about killing and eating live creatures. "This is so yummy!" Ginger exclaimed, "I wonder how that cow tastes." Ginger's blood lust grows with every bite he takes of flesh. The more he eats, the more he wants, and next the cow will be on the menu.

Ginger picks up the pace on eating the pig because he wishes to butcher the cow, the horse, and the fox. "You threaten me and I will gut you," Ginger said with a mouth full of pig intestines, "I will eat you and drink your milk as you die." Ginger could feel the urge to murder and eat coursing throughout his being, while the remaining blood and flesh devoured by Ginger dripped from his mouth. Once the pig's skeleton was picked clean, Ginger thought,

"I will save this for later." Ginger pulled the skeleton out of the shed and placed it next to the house. Then with his eyes set on the pasture, "You're next, cow."

Without Ginger knowing, Gretel woke up to get herself a drink of water and a snack. "Some fresh air would be nice," Gretel thought, "I'll go sit by the garden and relax." Gretel stepped out into the garden and looked on with horror at what Ginger was doing. "How could this be happening with my sweet little boy?" She quickly and quietly ran into the house in a blind panic. Gretel thought, "Did I do something wrong? I have to feed him something to curb his appetite before he eats all the livestock." Gretel looked through her cookbooks looking for a heavy and filling recipe that she could make. In a blind panic, she picked up the cookbook that started all this and just stared at it in a cold sweat.

Gretel suddenly freezes, staring blankly often to space, unable to move. A terrible memory falls upon her:

Vision blurry, unable to focus, all I could do is feel my hair being pulled as I was drug down the hall. The pain was excruciating but I couldn't move under my own power. The smell of urine, putrid flesh, and feces filling the air; it made me want to vomit. My lifeless body was like a rag doll being dragged around the house as if I was a children's toy. The old woman took in a deep breath through her nose and said, "smells like dinner, doesn't it? Don't worry your time is coming to an end." I couldn't respond, for my delirious state made me incapable to respond. I wanted to scream for help, but I couldn't control my body in any way. I remember my head dropping, hitting the floor, and suddenly my vision went in and out. I remember the old woman standing over me and she taunted me relentlessly. "You little bitch; you thought I was a sweet old lady. But you will find out what hell I will put you through before I eat your delicious flesh," cackled the old woman, "you know I could violate you and there's nothing you can do about it. It would be so easy and it would please me. Oh yes, very pleasurable in deed. Lucky for you I am just hungry, and you will make a fine meal."

I tried to talk and all of a sudden, I felt the sting of the old woman's hand. "Don't you dare fucking talk you little cunt, or I will have you slowly butchered. But I won't tell you how, for it is my fun secret," said the old woman. Then she opens a door and a rush of acrid smelling air hits me harder than she did. The smell was vile and it smelled like the hallway, but 100 times worse. I couldn't focus my eyes and I feared I was about to go blind. I could have sworn that this would be the end of me.

With a death grip handful of hair, the old woman had drugged me into a pitch black room across the slimy and cold floor. All I could think about was how this room was this dark, damp, and horrid. "This is your new home until I am ready to feast upon your fresh corpse," said the old woman, "this meal must go on without any restrictions. If you *do anything to fuck this up, your death will be slow, painful, and bloody. You will never forget me in the dark realm. "*

As I tried to mouth, "Fuck you," but before I got past "Fffff…" I felt the sting of her hand across my face again; followed by repeated kicks to my stomach and vagina. "Say it!" said the old woman, "say it! Talk back to me again and I will stomp your guts in until you shit out your organs. Do you understand me you little cunt?" All I could feel was pain and my eyes rolling around in my head. All I could do was keep quiet, try to rest, and come out of this torment alive. Before I blacked out, I felt my body dragged a few feet, head hit the floor, and something was slammed and locked behind me. I couldn't even cry from the pain. "Mommy…Daddy…why did you abandon me? You have forsaken me to this torment in which I may never survive. I hate you for what happens to me today. I hope you fall into the dark realm, you fuckers, and hope you suffer for what you did to me," is what ran through my mind. Then darkness fell on me……..

*Gretel suddenly snaps back into reality and suddenly needs to vomit. She runs to the outhouse, opens the door, and before she has a chance to aim her face into the outhouse toilet she has an explosion of bile, blood, and chunks of flesh all over the back wall of the outhouse. As Gretel continues to violently vomit her back contracts in pain and she begins to lose strength. "How can this be happening?" She questioned, "I never did anything wrong." Suddenly

Gretel felt as if her stomach had been stomped in and stabbed again. She continued to vomit, blood, and body matter. She continued to feel the sting of this literal gut wrenching experience for over the course of a few hours.

When the sickness finally ran its course, Gretel went to the well and fetched some water. She was dehydrated, light headed, and in excruciating pain. She had serious illnesses in the past but nothing compares to the hell she experienced. "I would rather have my skin peeled off my face than to ever go through that again,' said Gretel, "I'll just sit, read my favorite book, drink my water, and recuperate. So she took the pale of water inside the house and poured some into a glass. Then in no time she was sitting in her chair, drinking a cool glass of water, and reading her favorite book. She finally started to feel better and drift off into a world of her own.

The mid-morning sun continues to rise into the sky and the birds are singing. Ginger looked out into the pasture and saw the horse galloping, running, and trotting gracefully. "What a majestic sight," thought Ginger, "I bet he is delicious." The more life forms Ginger consumes, the more he wants and lusts after. Ginger then looks around and sees a lonely tree in the pasture. "Perfect," thought Ginger, "I'll hide in the tree." Ginger grabbed his hatchet and ran through the tall grass towards the tree. But without realizing it, Ginger was up wind from the horse." As Ginger made his way through the tall grass, the horse heard the rustling in the distance. The horse is now on high alert and spots the unnatural movement in the grass.

Chapter 9 – Horse's Last Ride

The horse, like all of the animals thus far, started off as a human being that has been cursed to be an animal. The horse was once a hard-working man by the name of John Shanemeyer, who used to work for Harold Hoggbottom as a laborer. Shanemeyer worked himself to death to provide for his wife Hillary, to whom he loved to no end. Both were honest hard-working people and they prided themselves on that. Hoggbottom had two classifications of workers: laborers and slaves. Laborers could go home, are free people, and are paid a wage. Slaves on the other hand are not free, are never paid, and are treated very poorly. Because Shanemeyer out ranked the slaves, he even had some that worked directly for him. He watched his slaves very closely and not necessarily for security reasons. Because Shanemeyer works so much he was barely home to be with his wife. He would watch the slave women that worked directly for him undress and redress, while touching himself relentlessly.

Shanemeyer's sexuality became too much after a while because he was unable to get a proper release. He did not want to cheat on his wife; so he would masturbate constantly when he was alone. But soon, that became too boring and he did not want to rape any women, children, or men because he loved his wife so much. So he began sexually molesting the horses because the horses don't speak. So weeks go by and this becomes quite disgusting to him. As Shanemeyer sexual frustration rises violently, he sets his sights on the slave women. One day he takes just one slave woman out to the stables to "assist him". Shanemeyer begins to sexually assault the slave women one by one, and is enjoying it a little too much. He would threaten them with death or physical punishment beyond what Hoggbottom would ever do to them.

The one woman Shanemeyer hasn't sexually assaulted, harmed, or realized was observing this happening was also planning a fate worse than death for him. This woman also was planning the same fate for Hoggbottom, for her past is quite dark.

One day she decides to seduce Shanemeyer and take him to the empty stall in the stable. The night before she had gathered some black ginger root she acquired from a traveling salesman. The salesman could tell she was in distress and it was not a good place. He handed the ginger root to her in an elongated glass cylinder so she could hide it from Hoggbottom inside her body. She inserted the elongated glass cylinders into her vagina, deep in her vagina to avoid detection.

Once she had Shanemeyer in the empty stall in the stable, she began to seduce Shanemeyer. Once the woman had him in a false sense of security, she turned around and squatted down to remove the glass cylinder from her vagina. Once she had removed the cylinder, she stood up, faced Shanemeyer with a seductive smile and evil in her eyes. Before she could take off one article of clothing, she threw the cylinder into Shanemeyer's face. Upon impact on the bridge of Shanemeyer's nose, the cylinder exploded, the powder inside burst all over Shanemeyer's face, and the glass slashed his face. As the blood began to drip down his face, the black ginger root began to soak into his bloodstream. The woman looked at him with her eyes beginning to glow red and she said, "for all those you have harmed, for all those you have defiled, I curse you and sentence you to a lifetime of suffering. Black ginger root hear my command and transform him to the animal in which he harmed the most." Shanemeyer began to feel sharp pains in his face and very quickly shot down his body all the way to his toes. His transformation had begun to transform into a horse, and it was going to be a long painful process. As it is, bones broke and reassembled, growing much larger than what he had before; his muscle and flesh torn to shreds, and reassembled to become a horse. Nearing the end of his transformation Shanemeyer, blacked out from the pain, but could still feel it in his nightmare.

The next day, this transformation was complete and the trauma of what had happened raised his memory of his past life. Soon he was being loaded onto a wagon with a pig. The horse had no idea what kind of hell he was about to endure for he had no memory, no recollection of his past life.

Soon the horse and the pig were joined by a goose and a cow on the wagon. They are being transported off to be sold or traded as livestock always is. All of them began to talk and the cow and the horse realized they were lovers in a past life. They had vowed to stick together no matter what happened. Little did they know they didn't have to put much effort into it for they were brought to a small house on the edge of the Mystic Forest to be traded. They were released into the pasture where they now live the rest of their lives.

Present day

"What is that?" thought the horse, "better not be a predator. I will crush them like the goose's head yesterday." The horse doesn't break visual of the disturbance in the distance but suddenly smells a familiar smell. "Hmmmm," the horse said, "what is that delicious little bastard doing out here?" The horse licks his lips, "you're mine now. Nothing will stand in my way." The horse slowly trots menacingly towards Ginger to clamp his teeth around him. The horse continues to creep towards Ginger with malice coursing through his veins. Then suddenly Ginger hears the light thuds of the horse's hooves coming steadily towards him. Ginger makes a sudden dash for the tree, "I can make it," said Ginger, "he can't catch me." The horse makes a mad dash at Ginger, "GET BACK HERE," demanded the horse, "I eat nothing but grass and grains. Let me taste you, delicious morsel!"

Ginger finds an opening in the tree's roots and sprints inside. The horse, with his sights on Ginger, who was just a couple yards from the tree, dug his hooves into the dirt and tried to stop. The horse turns to avoid the tree, but was going too fast, and trips over a protruding root in the ground. The horse's body turned and he fell on his side with a mighty thud, and hit his head on a rock sticking up out of the ground. Though in agony, the horse quickly tried to stand up, but fell back on his stomach. Blood rolling down his face, unable to see, unable to stand, the horse is in a blind panic. "Where are you," screamed the horse, "I want to eat you! Be a good little morsel and climb into my mouth." With the hatchet in hand, Ginger slowly maneuvers his way out from under the tree's roots. The horse catches a whiff of Ginger and begins savagely chomping towards the scent. "I can smell you! Get in my mouth! You are pissing me off," cried the horse, "I will get you!"

Ginger climbed the tree as quickly as he could and positioned himself on the first branch he could reach. The horse, still not able to stand, shuffled along the ground following Ginger's scent. He sniffed the ground up to the tree, opened his jaws, and crunched down on the tree trunk where Ginger's scent was strongest. With all his strength and fury, the horse embedded his teeth in the trunk of the tree, and was now a prisoner to the tree's mercy.

Ginger slunk down the tree trunk menacingly toward the horse. He stops just inches away from the horse's eyes, slowly looks up, tilts his head to the side, and smiles. "Hey Horsey," said Ginger. The horse responds with fear in his eyes, "Wha…What?"

"Now horsey, I cannot fit this hatchet in your mouth. I am going to open your mouth wider and break your teeth," said Ginger. The horse was too weak to react and could feel his life slip away slowly. Then suddenly the horse felt his face slashed from the mouth opening to his jaw bone. Ginger took the hatchet and golf swung the blade across the horse's cheek. The horse could only stay still and take the pain. The pain was excruciating but the horse was too weak to react. Then the horse felt a blow to his teeth. His upper and lower jaws were being destroyed by Ginger. The teeth and skull fragments began to build in the back of the horse's throat. The horse tries to swallow but is too weak to swallow. "I like you Horsey. You don't complain like the other animals," Said Ginger, "sorry Horsey, I cannot fit my hatchet through all the teeth in your mouth. I'll just slice off your flesh little bits at a time and eat you."

The horse's heart stops and he exhales on last time. The horse had finally died from his inflicted brutal wounds from his attacker. Ginger slicing bits of flesh and enjoying the taste of lean meat. "Horsey, I don't know if you can hear me, but you are delicious. Best meal I have had yet today," said Ginger. A few hours go by and Ginger is over half way done picking the bones clean, and begins to eat the innards of the horse. As Ginger continues to devour the horse, he notices the cow in the distance. The cow was peacefully grazing in the pasture and enjoying the warmth from the sun.

        "I better hurry," said Ginger, "I don't want her to catch me." A breeze picks up and Ginger is standing upwind from the cow and the cow begins to pick up Ginger's scent. The cow picks up her head and begins walking towards the delicious scent. Ginger gets behind the tree so he's out of sight of the cow. He notices an opening in the roots and climbs underneath. "I certainly hope she doesn't see me in here," said Ginger. Step-by-step she grows more and more anxious and hungry. "I know that smell," said the cow, "that delicious walking little thing I saw earlier." The cow began to pick up the pace as the sand got stronger, but suddenly she stopped at the site of a skeleton of the horse. "Oh my creator," exclaimed the cow, "Horse? Is that you? This cannot be happening right now." The cow begins to weep for her fallen lover. Even though they were two different species, the cow was madly in love with the horse. In fact, the horse and cow were going to try to make a cross-species abomination. But their evening of breeding never came to be. "My love, I will avenge you. I vow this to you my fallen love," said the cow.

Chapter 10 – Cow's Revenge

The cow used to be a loyal woman to her husband, John Shanemeyer. Her name was Hillary and she stood by her husband John for many years despite his employer. She loathed Harold Hoggbottom because she knew what he did to women. Because they needed income she just looked the other way and continued to support her husband. One day Hillary went to visit John at work and found out that he was in the stables. Once Hillary arrived at the stables, she saw that John was with another woman. Hillary's jealousy and her insecurities took over and she followed them. As the sexual nature of these two being together began to get steamier, Hillary was overcome with rage. Before she could do anything, she noticed the woman John was with took something out of her vagina and threw it into his face. At that point, Hillary attacked the woman to protect her husband. The woman noticed that Hillary was running at her so the woman took action. She quickly dipped her nails into John's blood and slashed Hillary across the face. "Fuck you, you cow," said the woman, "you will meet the same fate as this man for what you attempted to do." Like the horse, she was going to be traded off as her new life as a cow," said the woman. Before she knew it, Hillary had transformed into a cow and was on a small property outside of the Mystic Forest to live out the rest of her days. Like her husband John, Hillary has no recollection of their past life together, other than they were in love.

Present Day

The cow suddenly grew with rage and began to violently jerk her body around searching for Ginger. "Get out here you little shit. I know you killed Horse," exclaimed the cow, "I'm going to crush you and then lick you up, little by little, just so I can hear you whimper." The cow continued to look around but could not see where Ginger was located. The call grows increasingly violent and angry. 'I'm going to enjoy devouring your flesh," yelled the cow, "your crunchy, little body inside my mouth as I slowly crunch down on you and listen to you scream in agony."

Ginger positions himself with the cow insight and positions his hatchet, ready to strike. The cow begins to walk around the tree where Ginger was located and smells the tree. "I know you're close. I demand you show yourself." Ginger postures and just as the cow looks away from him, Ginger runs out and slices the cows utter from front to back, right down the middle . The cow's milk begins to flow out of her utter mixed with blood. The cow begins to panic and whales uncontrollably in pain. Ginger moves off to the right slightly, then runs full force at the cow and slices the cow's stomach wide open. The cow's innards dropped to the ground, steam rolling off the innards, and the cow suddenly fainted.

The cow suddenly comes to and sees Ginger just inches away from her eye. The cow is extremely weak at this point from the blood loss from her utter and stomach. Ginger peers into the eye of the cow and says, "I'm going to let you join the horse in the dark realm. Maybe there you'll realize your mistake taunting me or threatening me." Ginger lifts the hatchet up, draws back, and swings with all his might, landing the hatchet into one of the protruding roots of the nearby tree. "I am not going to kill you with my hatchet," said Ginger, "I'm going to eat you alive." The cow is so weak she can only wait to see what was going to happen next. Ginger jumped on the cow's head, walked towards her stomach, and began eating the cow's flesh through the incision he had made. The cow can't even scream at this point; all she can do is wait for death to flow through her. As Ginger consumes every part of the cow, the cow regrets her choice to threaten Ginger, and she begins to succumb to her wounds and pain .

As her body runs cold, the cow begins losing feeling in her body, and begins seeing a darkness blackout the landscape. She can feel chunks of her flesh being ripped from her body, she tears up and remembers life before they curse. She and her husband would spend time together and plan their future together. They planned to have a large family with four or five children and maybe have a nice farm. But now, it is no longer within their grasp. With a final exhale, the cow dies from shock and blood loss.

Ginger is slowly munching away at the cow and humming a tune he made up. "cow," said Ginger, "you were very pretty and you are very tasty. The

horse was not as tasty as you." Then Ginger sings an innocent sounding, but deranged, song about the cow,
"

cow.

Delicious cow.

You are so yummy.

Yum, yum, yum.

Yum, yum, yum.

MMMMMMM, yum.

With one final bite, the cow's flesh has been picked clean from the skeleton. "Bye cow," said Ginger, "thank you for a tasty meal. But I am still hungry and need to find something to eat. Ginger leaned over to the cow's skull and gave a gentle peck on the cheek bone. Instinct begins to kick in and Ginger begins setting a trap for the fox. While he was working he sang:

cow.

Delicious cow.

You are so yummy.

Yum, yum, yum.

Yum, yum, yum.

MMMMMMM, yum.

Chapter 11 – The Fox Strikes

The fox was the worst human that ever lived when he was human. He went by many names because he didn't want anybody to know who he truly was. His last known name was Theodore Featherbelt. He constantly stole money and other items of value that he just resold to make more money. One of Featherbelt's obsessions was to break into people's houses whether or not anybody is home because the adrenaline rush aroused him. If anyone was home, he proceeded to kill them and have his way with their dead corpses. Featherbelt had no boundaries when it came to breaking and entering someone's home. To him everything's a weapon and everything is disposable income. He knows people who practice black magic and will pay top dollar for human body parts. Featherbelt has occasionally ripped off practitioners of the dark arts and moved very quickly out of the area. But what he doesn't know is one of those practitioners had placed a hex on him, and cursed him to turn into an animal. So Featherbelt continued on with his life, not worried about any repercussions of his actions.

When he had a profitable week, he paid women for a weekend that he would dispose of; however, he felt was necessary. Occasionally Featherbelt would find men in their early 20s if he felt frisky, and they met the same fate as women did. Featherbelt got his pleasure in any means possible. When he felt he tapped an entire village or town, he would leave dead bodies and body parts of his victims, all over town in the most horrific fashion possible.

Featherbelt's shenanigans varied on one night on how he would decorate the town. He would hide people's heads in gardens to scare the elderly to death, placed fingers of hands wrapped around door knobs, placed human faces on various different livestock, even broke into people's houses and slip human feet inside of their shoes and boots. With whole bodies, Featherbelt would have the bodies posed in offensive gestures in front of people's houses, gardens, inside churches, and even in cemeteries. Bodies have been found around town with other human body parts inserted in them, such as arms, fingers, legs inserted into different orifices on display in the town square. Featherbelt has gone as far as placing the local priest on his back; legs spread wide open, getting fucked by another man in front of the Crucifix with Christ, crucified inside a church, while still dressed in his priest robe.

Featherbelt has tried to do what he considers, "artistic" with body parts and animals. He has visited local farms, stables, and ranches; and killed the livestock in order to insert human body parts into them to create another being. Smaller livestock were inserted into the bodies of dead people. There is no limit to this man's imagination because the more horrific he made it, the more excited he got.

One day during his escapades through a farmer's livestock, he began to feel very ill. His stomach began to turn and pain shot through his entire body relentlessly. The hex had finally completed under a full moon and he had been bitten by a rabid fox. Featherbelt had never felt such pain and agony ever in his life because he has never been caught before. The pain was so intense he blacked out for the rest of the night. As his body slowly changes in the moonlight, you can hear the cracking of his bones, the tearing of his skin, and flesh in the night. He dreamt that night of being tortured all over his body and he found no sexual pleasure in it.

When he finally came to consciousness the next morning, Featherbelt was being violated by the hillbilly farmer. "This is for killing my livestock you son of a bitch fox," said the hillbilly farmer, "I'm going to fuck you to death you little fucker." The hillbilly farmer had his hand wrapped around Featherbelt's fox-like throat and was raping him rectally. Once the fox regained his strength, he dug his claws into the dirt and pulled away quickly from the hillbilly farmer. The rage inside of the fox burned and he retaliated violently against the hillbilly farmer by biting off his genitals. The hillbilly farmer began to bleed profusely from his crotch and started to feel incredibly ill from the pain and the rabies. Then the fox disappeared without a trace until he found refuge outside of the mystic forest near a little cottage with an old man and woman residing there.

Night fall is upon the land and the fox is out hunting. Suddenly the fox picks up Ginger's scent, and moves in closer for the kill. The glint of the moonlight shined on a gingerbread man shaped thing leaning up against the tree. The fox lowers his stance and slowly creeps across the ground, going slowly and gracefully. "I now get to rape and consume you; my delicious little morsel," thought the fox, "you may have killed all those other retarded beasts, but you will never fool me." Inching closer and closer to his prey, salivating practically foaming at the mouth, body tensing up, and the fox makes a dash at the gingerbread man. Within a few short steps, the fox clamps his mighty jaws around the gingerbread man's head and crushes it to dust.

The fox begins to hack and cough violently, for he just ate a diversion made of dust, mud, and sticks. Ginger is waiting in a tree by the river, ready to bear the hatchet into the fox's skull. The fox stands still and Ginger jumps from the branch of the tree, swings his hatchet downward, and strikes the fox on the skull with the blunt side of the hatchet. The fox's skull is cracked open, but he is still alive. The fox's body drops to the ground and begins to spasm. "What the hell?" said Ginger, "the sharp side of the hatchet was to go into your skull. How did I make a mistake?" Ginger paused for a moment and then had an idea. "Come with me," said Ginger grabbing the fox's tail and dragging him towards the house, I have the perfect end for you. You sick fuck."

Ginger dragged the fox for several hundred feet back to the house. The fox is still unable to move under his own power. "Stay here," Ginger said sarcastically, "I'll be back." The fox tried to move his legs but no luck. All of a sudden, a large, flickering light appeared on the other side of the house. "Come on," said Ginger, "I am hungry." Ginger dragged the fox over to a very large fire with a spit assembly in place. Ginger picked up a large metal object and dragged it over so the fox could see what he was doing. "You threatened to rape and eat me. Well I am not going to rape you, but about as close as I will get to since I have no way to do it. Do try to relax, and remember don't clench." The fox was very uncomfortable and puzzled at the cryptic threat placed upon him. While the fox is faced away from the fire, Ginger raises the spit, takes aim, then rams the spit into the fox's anus, scraping it against his spine, and out the fox's mouth. The fox had never felt such pain and was unable to scream for mercy. Then with impossible strength, Ginger lifts the spit, with the fox on, and slams it across the spit assembly, holding the fox in the open flames.

The fox's hair is quickly burned off his body, flesh begins to char, and the pain is excruciating. The fox, in his final moments, relives all the horrible things he has done. The gruesome killings that he did for fun, the rape of many animals in the forest, and the lives he destroyed. A single tear rolls out of his right eye as he inhales his last breath of air with flames engulfing his lungs. Ginger looks on frowning and breathing heavily. "I will enjoy eating you," Ginger said to the fox as he dies on a spit, "I will enjoy slicing your dick off and eating it first. I will take away your rape tool."

As the flames die off, Ginger has been slicing off piece after piece of the fox's body and consuming them. Laughing as he ate the fox, "How's does it feel to be defeated by a cookie? Huh? Oh yeah, you're dead. I hope you are getting raped in the other world." Harboring much resentment towards the fox, Ginger chopped at the chard corpse of the fox violently. As the burnt flesh flies all over the yard and Ginger laughs sadistically. Then Ginger kicks the spit assembly over and the fox's remains roll across the ground. Ginger approaches the dead lifeless remains of the fox and finishes the body; bones and flesh.

Ginger took the last of the fox's flesh and consumed it. The fox was no more and Ginger was still hungry. "I ate one fox and three large fucking animals today! How am I still hungry?!?!" Ginger yelled furiously. An owl called out in the night with a screech. Startled, Ginger grabbed the spit and hurled it in the direction the sound came from. The owl began another call and it stopped as fast as it began. Ginger had thrown the spit through the owl's mouth and out the back of its skull, thus pinning it to the tree. With a few nerve impulses, the owl's body twists and contorts for a few brief moments; the owl becomes still and lifeless. Frustrated and alone, Ginger walked back into the house to go to bed. He was exhausted from his long day, and despite his hunger, he wanted nothing to eat.

Chapter 12 – Hanzel's Encounter

As Hanzel knows, be on alert at all times; because there is no telling what creatures he may encounter. But as he travels onward he gathers berries, edible grubs, and other tasty insects. "The overgrowth is thicker than I remember," said Hanzel, "well this forest isn't explored much." So Hanzel continued on his journey through the Mystic Forest.

Suddenly, Hanzel is alerted to a faint sound in the far distance and he stops to listen carefully. "What was that?" Hanzel whispered to himself, "Better see what that was." He followed the sound, and as he got closer, his stomach began to knot up. With each step, his anxiety got higher because his intuition was telling him 'turn around' and he ignored it. His steps became slower and his footsteps became softer. What little Hanzel knew is that his life was now in grave danger.

Off to his right, he heard a sharp 'squeal' only a stone's throw away. The gut wrenching sound of bones crunching and snapping, flesh being ripped from a corpse, and the ungodly sight of the largest wolf Hanzel had ever seen within killing distance. Hanzel's body went cold, for he knew this wasn't an ordinary wolf. This wolf stood on its hind legs over 8 feet tall, muscular body, razor sharp claws, powerful jaws, and could speak. "Little pig, little pig let me in," said the wolf mockingly, "Then I will tear your house and you apart." The wolf was talking to something, but Hanzel couldn't see what it was.

Then suddenly it became clear when the wolf turned around. The wolf was using the severed head of a pig it killed just moments before Hanzel stumbled upon him as a puppet. "That stupid pig in the brick house doesn't stand a chance," said the wolf, "I will rape and kill his sows and leave the heads on his front lawn. I will taste his fear, torment, and drink his tears when he gives in to his anguish." The wolf was getting aroused at the thought of the torment of the last pig.

A gentle breeze picks up, brushes by Hanzel and glides to the wolf. The wolf suddenly stops as he picks up the scent of a human. His pupils shrink, his mouth waters, and he begins to growl. The wolf drops the sow's head and he sniffs to find the source of the smell. "This human is close," said the wolf, "I can smell them." As the wolf tracks the smell, Hanzel's heart is racing. "Shit, that fucking wolf has my scent," said Hanzel, "that thing is going to maul me to death or even eat me alive." Either way this wasn't going to be good for Hanzel.

The wolf is now within slashing distance of Hanzel and the only thing between them is a bush. Neither one can see each other…yet. The wolf creeps up towards the bush, postures to strike, jaws ready to crush the throat of the victim, and then…. "Get out there and see if he is still there," shouted the last pig in the distance. The wolf said, "I'll deal with you later. Whoever you are." Then the wolf ran off toward the pig's property.

Hanzel vomited violently. Relieved to be alive, Hanzel continued to vomit and reflect on what just happened. "That was too close," said Hanzel, "but I did promise my bride a wild pig." Hanzel continued on his hunt. Little did Hanzel realize that the wolf never forgets a scent.

Hanzel hunts for a few days and the only pigs he encountered were all mauled and eaten in horrific scenes of a massacre. Houses destroyed, blood paints the area, and looks of horror on the faces left behind. Never did Hanzel ever imagine this would come to any living creature. "You know, my wife is very understanding," thought Hanzel, "I will butcher the pig in the pasture and we will have a delicious feast in her honor. I can get another one from a traveler, I am sure. If not I have other animals to eat." Hanzel gathered some supplies left at the destroyed houses and started his journey back home.

Hanzel kept getting the sneaking suspicion that he was being followed. Rustling leaves and brush followed Hanzel and there was no wind. Every creature was quiet and watching as if they knew something was going on. Hanzel was very uncomfortable and kept wondering, "What is going on? Why are all the woodland creatures quiet? Are they going to attack me? What do they know that I don't?" These creatures only moved their heads to follow Hanzel's movement. Then as Hanzel moved farther down the path towards his home, the animals began to follow. The way the animals were reacting was as if it was a public execution. "My goodness this is just silly," said Hanzel, "ok little friends. You may head home now." The animals began bob their heads up, then down, up then down, and up then down. "This display was not typical animal behavior," thought Hanzel, "what is that sound?" The birds began to do a singing chant going from high note, to low note with 3 seconds each: high...low...high...low...high...low, and that kept repeating. The deer stomped their left front hoof, then the right, with 3 seconds in between: left stomp...right stomp... left stomp...right stomp...left stomp...right stomp, and kept repeating. The squirrels in the trees had rocks and followed a beat as well. The squirrels found hollow branches and knocked the rhythm: knock...knock.knock...knock...knock.knock...knock ...knock.knock, and kept repeating.

Hanzel began to run towards home as fast as he could but he was still over 3 hours walk from home. "I have to run," said Hanzel, "something is wrong with the creatures." His adrenaline kicked into overdrive, and he began running like a sprinter. He looked back and dozens of animals were following him, and oddly enough, staying behind him. At no point in time did they make a pass, or attempt to stop him. It was as if they were following him to see what was going to happen to him. Then Hanzel noticed off to his right, a shadowy figure was running alongside him, keeping pace. Two red eyes flash in Hanzel's direction and the shadowy figure drops down as if disappearing. Then with a growl on Hanzel's left, the shadowy figure appears again. "Is that the same creature?" asked Hanzel, "this thing moves faster than I do. SHIT!" With all the hurdles and obstacles before him, Hanzel pushes on with all his might.

Again the shadowy figure disappears, but this time without a trace. "What the hell?" Hanzel exclaimed, "Where the fuck did it go?" Hanzel was very uneasy because the woodland creatures began their chant again. This time they were more aggressive about it and crept closer with each sound they made. Hanzel starts running again, but quickly begins running out of energy for he had been running for untold amounts of time. It seemed like he had been running for days and he was about to lose all hope when he suddenly saw the lights from his home. He pushed as hard as he could, just feet from the edge of the Mystic Forest until he collapsed. He crawled on his stomach trying to get out of the forest but his energy levels were almost nothing. Barely able to breathe, he tries to summon the strength to stand and fails many times. But he wasn't going to black out, he reached deep down, got on his hands and knees, and crawled as fast as he could. He thought he had a good pace, but in all reality he was barely moving. His whole body was shaking and he could barely hold up his head. Suddenly he realized he was inches away from his garden.

Exhausted from almost certain death, Hanzel finally sees the lights of his beautiful home in front of him. "I cannot wait to see Gretel," Hanzel said to himself, "she is an understanding woman and she will be glad to know that I made it home alive." He hears rustling in close proximity to him and he stops. "Who is there?" Shouted Hanzel, "I have a gun and I will shoot you. Get off my property!" A light growl sounded nearby and Hanzel froze in fear. "I remember you," said a deep deranged voice, "and I know your wife inside. It would be a shame if anything would happen to her before you die." Hanzel attempted to reach for his rifle but his arms were of no use, for he exhausted himself to nothing. It was getting dark quickly, and Hanzel was losing precious time.

"Soon you won't be able to see anything in here," said the voice again, "I am going to have some fun with you before I make your life a dying hell." Hanzel's senses began to heighten due to his adrenaline raging through his veins. He listens, scans the area, and he crawls slowly towards his house not knowing his end was near.

Inch by inch he becomes more optimistic. "I am going to survive," said Hanzel, "there's my house. As he steps on the edge of his garden, he feels a huge hand quickly wrap around his neck and the ground no longer under his hands and legs. A black, shadowy figure with glowing red eyes turns Hanzel so they are face to face. "You smell familiar," said the black, shadowy figure in a deep growling voice.

Hanzel drops his rifle as he is physically thrown back into the forest. Flying through the air, Hanzel feels a sudden sharp pain in his back. He landed on the right of his head, forcing his neck to break on a large root protruding out of the ground. Unable to stand, crawl, or escape, all Hanzel could do is wait to die. Hyperventilating, Hanzel struggles to breathe and feels extreme panic flow through his body. He suddenly realized it was the wolf that slaughtered the pigs.

Suddenly there was silence, only silence. Hanzel tried to look around to spot his attacker but no one was to be found with his limited movement. "What the hell?" Hanzel repeatedly said, "What the hell is going on? Where is that thing? What did I do to deserve this?" Suddenly, out of nowhere, he feels a warm, searing pain come over him in his chest. A wolf towered over Hanzel, but he cannot see them for his vision was fading. Unable to scream, Hanzel opened his mouth and exhaled out one final puff of air mixed with blood from his lungs. Motionless, Hanzel bled out and never knew his attacker. Eyes wide open, mouth partially open, and skin quickly losing pigment. The wolf moves in closer and says in a deep voice, "I bet you are delicious." The wolf takes its right pointer finger, exposing the claw, and drags the claw from Hanzel's neck to his belly button as if he was dissecting him. The black shadowy figure licks Hanzel's face and proceeds to break Hanzel's sternum with its mighty clawed hands and open him up like a book. The sound of Hanzel's rib cage snapping echoes throughout the Mystic Forest.

Gretel stepped out of the kitchen for some fresh air and saw something going in the forest. She could tell this wasn't any ordinary animal fight or self-defense. "This can wait in the over for a moment," said Gretel, "I better take care of this before it ends up on my doorstep." As she got closer, she saw Hanzel being mauled by the wolf. "Hanzel!" Gretel shouted, "Get the fuck away from him!" A gunshot suddenly frightens the wolf, and he bellows a deep roar at the rifleman. Gretel was standing at the edge of the Mystic Forest, barely able to see the wolf. She took aim with a rifle and fired at the wolf. The shot missed and hit a nearby tree behind the wolf. The wolf decided this was a fight for later time and ran away. Gretel ran over to Hanzel and she was distressed to see that Hanzel was mauled by a creature from the forest. "Oh my creator," Gretel said, "Hanzel, my darling! NO, CREATOR NO!" There was nothing she could do but watch his still beating heart come to a slow stop. "I will take you home to meet Ginger. He should know his noble father." Gretel dragged Hanzel to the house and brought him into the kitchen on the table. "I'll go get your son," said Gretel, "so he can at least see your face." She covered him with a black sheet from the neck down and searched for Ginger.

Gretel's skin was very dry and brittle and she was getting worried. She had made up a special skin crème to help with that and she will put some on later. She stepped back outside and called out for Ginger, "GINGER! Ginger, come home honey! Time to eat!" Ginger came walking up to the house looking very unhappy. "What is wrong sweetheart?" asked

Gretel. "Momma, I have eaten all the animals in the pasture. The goose, pig, horse, and cow but I am still hungry. I am sorry I did that but my tummy was hurting until I ate them," said Ginger. Gretel looked out into the pasture and saw 3 large animal corpses. "Oh my," said Gretel, "You were busy, weren't you?" Ginger thought he was going to be punished for what he had done, but he realized that his mommy still loved him very much. "Come inside," said Gretel, "I want you to meet your father." Ginger looked at her and asked, "Father? What's a father?" Gretel embarrassed and disappointed in herself that she never explained that Hanzel was a father to Ginger. "Well in most families there is a mommy and a daddy. Your daddy was hunting for a wild pig for dinner but he was gone so long that I forgot about him." Ginger got excited and jumped up and down as he walked, "Where is daddy? I want to hug him." Gretel didn't know how to tell Ginger what had happened. "You daddy is on the table right there but he isn't alive." Ginger stopped jumping and with a horrified look on his face, stared at Gretel.

Gretel's voice was becoming quickly scratchy, her skin was flaking off her body, and her face was wilting. Her whole demeanor changed as time went on. "Come my child," Gretel said in a scratchy voice, "I'll show you him." Gretel picked up Ginger and placed him on Hanzel's chest. Ginger wanted to feel sad, but a violent urge came over him. Ginger could feel the blood soaked sheet under his feet and it took him back to when he ate all the animals. Ginger grabbed hold of the sheet and pulled it back exposing

Hanzel's freshly murdered corpse. He looked at Gretel and she simply nodded in approval.

Ginger began to eat Hanzel's flesh and began eating him from the inside out. Gretel was getting sexually aroused watching her former husband being eaten by a pastry. She begins rubbing her breasts and realizes that her flesh flaked off more and more as she rubbed her body. She moves her right hand down to her pussy and begins to masturbate violently while her son devours her dead husband's corpse. The more she touched herself the more skin flakes came off her body. Little did she know, her body has transformed into a monstrosity of her former self. She continued to pleasure herself and even walked over to the black sheet covered in blood and rubbed it on her intimate parts. She even rang out the sheet, blood dripped into her mouth, and ran down her body.

Several minutes had passed and Ginger had just finished eating the last of Hanzel's flesh and crawled out the bottom of the rib cage. "Mommy," Ginger said, "I am full and I cannot eat another bite." Ginger finally knew what feeling full felt like and he loved it. He looked around and his mommy was nowhere to be seen. Ginger was so tired that he sat on the table to rest. Then suddenly a dark shadowy creature appeared in front of him. "Who are you?" asked Ginger, "Where my mommy?" A match lit up out of nowhere revealing the creature's identity. "Mommy," Ginger said with a sigh of relief, "daddy was delicious. Where did you go?"

But an odd sound filled the room. It is the sound of leather tearing and it was coming from Gretel's face. She bit her bottom lip and began to consume her own skin. Ginger looked on in horror and realized that mommy wasn't the same lady she was before. Bite by bite, Gretel's face disappears into her mouth. "Mommy! What are you doing? Mommy!" Ginger said in a blind panic. With a quick slurp, Gretel's human skin was devoured and she revealed what she had become…a Gingerbread woman. Ginger was hesitant but was excited because his mommy looked like him. She reached down to stroke his little cookie face, not saying a word. "I love you mommy," said Ginger, "it can be just you and me forever." Gretel smiled and with a deep scratchy voice responded, "Well…you are partly right." She pulls out a knife she had holstered, raised it toward the ceiling, blade shining in the candle light of the home. "Mommy?" asked Ginger, "What are you doing?" Without saying a word, she decapitates Ginger's head from his body. Ginger's body goes limp and quickly hardens into a crunchy cookie and his head stays alive. With fear and panic in his face, Ginger watches Gretel slowly eat his crunchy body. She bites off the limbs, munches the torso, all the while, moaning with extreme pleasure.

Finally, Gretel picks up the dying head of Ginger, places it into her mouth, and slowly bites down; crushing Ginger's head. He tries to scream, but nothing comes out. All that could be seen, is his mouth moving frantically as Gretel's cookie jaws slowly close. Ginger feels darkness waft over him as his head crumbles to dust in Gretel's mouth. She chews and swallows her only child. Gretel wipes off her mouth and then she turns to look inside her oven to reveal another gingerbread man.

The End

Printed in Great Britain
by Amazon

61554012R00069